Nain Rouge
The Red Legend

CALIBER
COMICS

Nain Rouge
The Red Legend

A Folkteller Tale
www.folktellertales.com

CALIBER
COMICS
www.calibercomics.com

Nain Rouge

The Red Legend

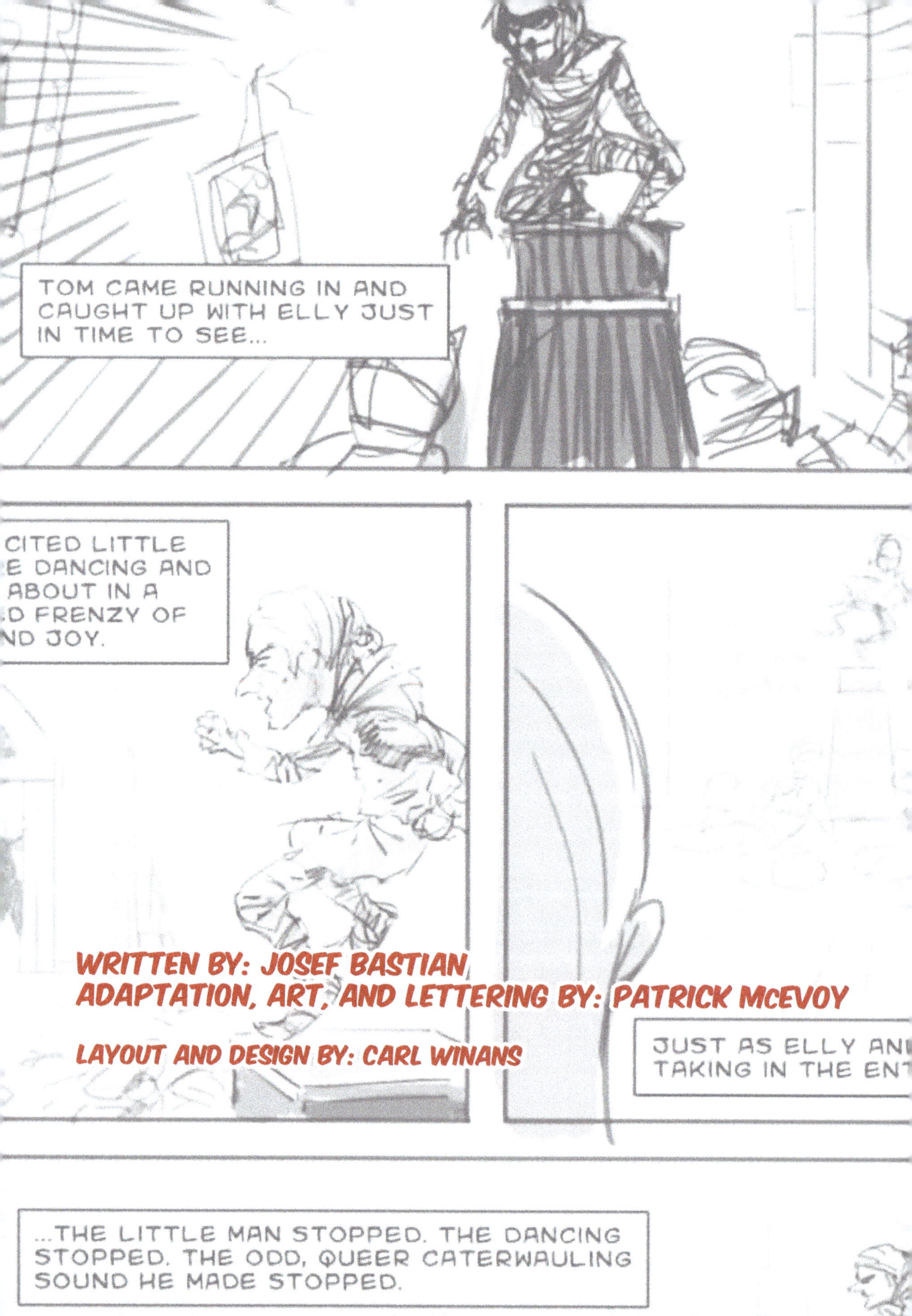

TOM CAME RUNNING IN AND CAUGHT UP WITH ELLY JUST IN TIME TO SEE...
CITED LITTLE E DANCING AND ABOUT IN A D FRENZY OF ND JOY.
WRITTEN BY: JOSEF BASTIAN
ADAPTATION, ART, AND LETTERING BY: PATRICK McEVOY
LAYOUT AND DESIGN BY: CARL WINANS
JUST AS ELLY AN TAKING IN THE ENT
...THE LITTLE MAN STOPPED. THE DANCING STOPPED. THE ODD, QUEER CATERWAULING SOUND HE MADE STOPPED.

CHAPTER 1

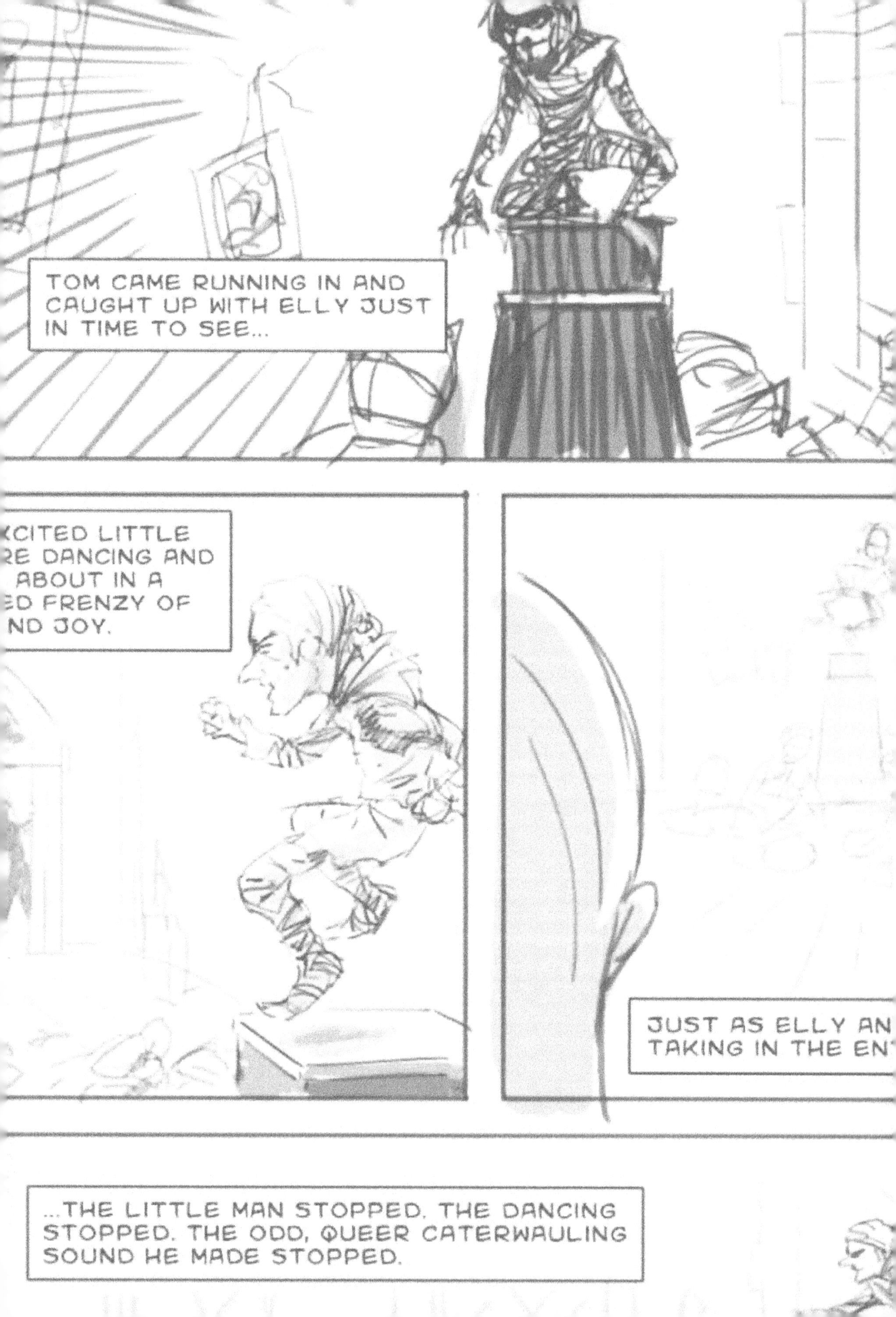

TOM CAME RUNNING IN AND
CAUGHT UP WITH ELLY JUST
IN TIME TO SEE...

XCITED LITTLE
RE DANCING AND
ABOUT IN A
ED FRENZY OF
ND JOY.

JUST AS ELLY AN
TAKING IN THE EN

...THE LITTLE MAN STOPPED. THE DANCING
STOPPED. THE ODD, QUEER CATERWAULING
SOUND HE MADE STOPPED.

THE MUSEUM FELT VERY DIFFERENT TODAY. ELLY AND TOM BOTH NOTICED IT. THE BEST FRIENDS HAD BEEN TO THE DETROIT INSTITUTE OF ARTS ON FIELD TRIPS MANY, MANY TIMES, AND HAD NEVER HAD SUCH A CREEPY, EERIE FEELING...
...YOU WILL SEE RIVERA USES THE IMAGE OF A BABY GROWING IN THE BULB OF A PLANT.
THIS WAS DONE TO REMIND US THAT ALL HUMAN ENDEAVORS ARE ROOTED IN THE EARTH, THE WATER AND THE LAND ON WHICH WE LIVE.
IT WAS NOT QUITE A SMELL OR A SOUND OR SOMETHING THEY SAW. NO, IT WAS MORE LIKE A WHISPER, A HINT, A SHADOW. A FEELING DOWN DEEP IN YOUR SOUL THAT SOMETHING WAS NOT QUITE RIGHT.
COULD YOU IMAGINE HOW LONG IT TOOK TO PAINT THESE?
SLOPPING ALL THAT PAINT ON A WALL, I WOULD HAVE BEEN BORED OUT OF MY MIND. KIND OF LIKE I AM NOW!
STOP COMPLAINING! A LITTLE CULTURE WOULDN'T KILL YOU, TOMMY.

I DON'T KNOW, IT MIGHT!

ELLY COULD HAVE SWORN THAT THERE WAS A SHADOW MOVING, APPEARING AND DISAPPEARING, SHIFTING BEHIND THE INDUSTRIAL IMAGES AND UNFAMILIAR FACES WITHIN THE PAINTING.
SHE COULD CATCH A GLIMPSE OF IT WITH HER PERIPHERAL VISION, BUT AS SOON AS SHE WOULD TURN AND FOCUS, LIKE A WISP OF SMOKE...

...IT WAS GONE!
INSTINCTIVELY, ELLY RAN BACK INTO THE MAIN HALL.
CRRASH!
KA-WAM!
KLANGG!

BEFORE THE FINAL ECHO FADED, ELLY SAW SOMETHING EVEN MORE UNBELIEVABLE...
CRASH!

AT THE FAR END OF THE HALL WHERE THE 17TH CENTURY ITALIAN CORSALETTO ARMOR ONCE STOOD, CROUCHED A SMALL, GNARLED, BIZZARE-LOOKING CREATURE.
TOM CAME RUNNING IN AND CAUGHT UP WITH ELLY JUST IN TIME TO SEE...

...THIS EXCITED LITTLE *CREATURE* DANCING AND JUMPING ABOUT IN A MADDENED FRENZY OF ANGER AND JOY.

JUST AS ELLY AND TOM WERE TAKING IN THE ENTIRE SCENE...

...THE LITTLE MAN *STOPPED*. THE DANCING STOPPED. THE ODD, QUEER CATERWAULING SOUND HE MADE STOPPED.
EVERYTHING STOPPED.

...EXCEPT HIS *EYES*.

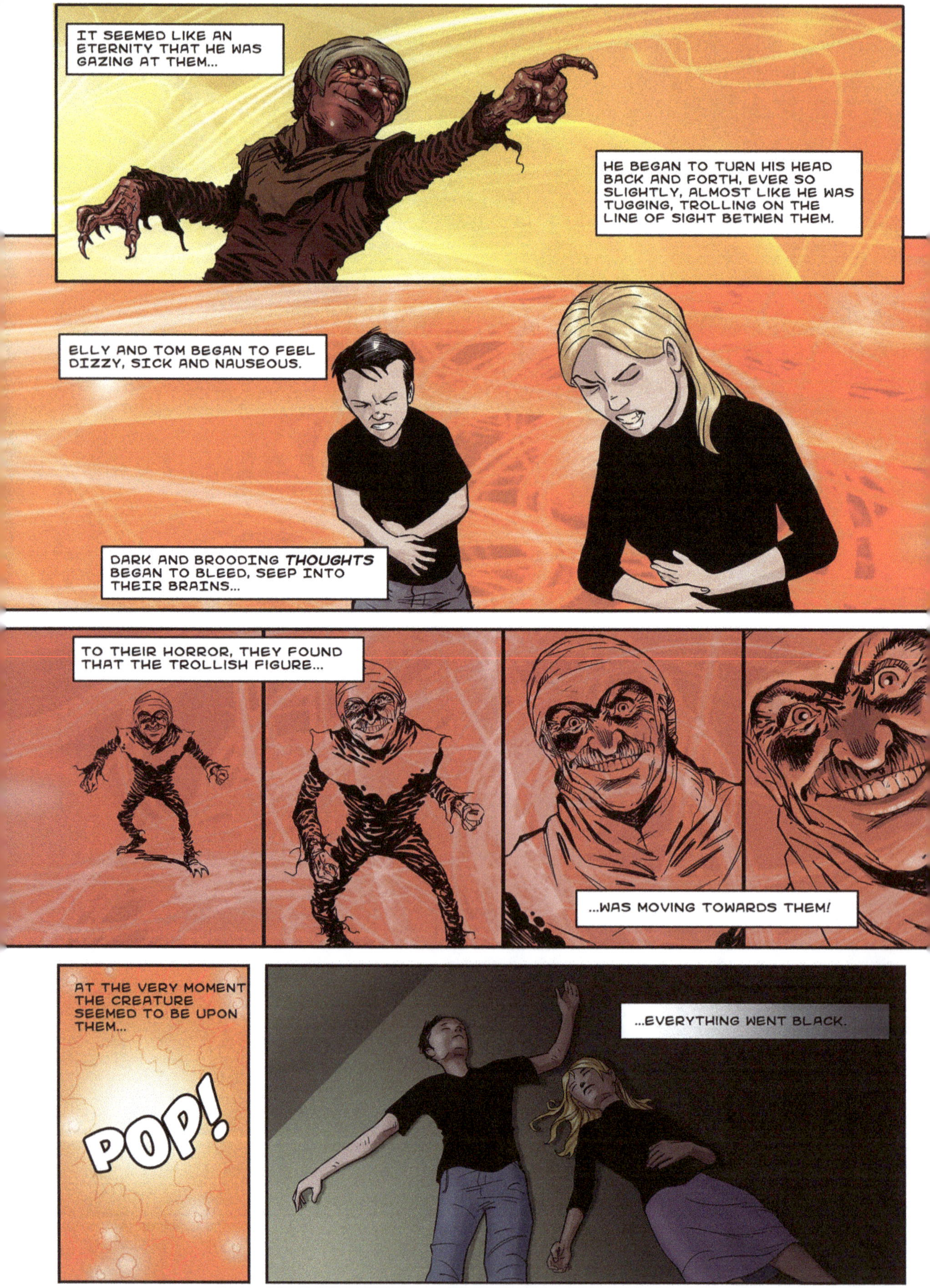

IT SEEMED LIKE AN ETERNITY THAT HE WAS GAZING AT THEM...
HE BEGAN TO TURN HIS HEAD BACK AND FORTH, EVER SO SLIGHTLY, ALMOST LIKE HE WAS TUGGING, TROLLING ON THE LINE OF SIGHT BETWEN THEM.
ELLY AND TOM BEGAN TO FEEL DIZZY, SICK AND NAUSEOUS.
DARK AND BROODING THOUGHTS BEGAN TO BLEED, SEEP INTO THEIR BRAINS...
TO THEIR HORROR, THEY FOUND THAT THE TROLLISH FIGURE...
...WAS MOVING TOWARDS THEM!

AT THE VERY MOMENT THE CREATURE SEEMED TO BE UPON THEM...
POP!

...EVERYTHING WENT BLACK.

CHILDREN! CHILDREN! ARE YOU OK?

DID ANYONE GET THE LICENSE PLATE NUMBER OF THAT TRUCK THAT HIT US?
WHAT HAPPENED?

WE WERE HOPING THAT YOU COULD TELL US!
I'M NOT SURE WHAT HAPPENED, REALLY. I RAN IN HERE WHEN I HEARD ALL THE NOISE, AND THE NEXT THING I KNEW...

I WAS RUNNING IN AFTER ELLY TO SEE WHERE SHE HAD GONE. WHEN I GOT INTO THE MAIN HALL I SAW HER STARING AT A P--

OW!

UM...WHAT I WAS SAYING, WAS THAT WHEN I CAME IN, I SAW ELLY STARING AT A PILE OF ARMOR.

WELL, WELL, IT LOOKS LIKE WE'VE HAD QUITE A HANDS-ON FIELD TRIP THIS MORNING.
I CAN ASSURE YOU SIR, THAT NONE OF MY STUDENTS HAD ANYTHING TO DO WITH THIS TERRIBLE MESS.
IN FACT, IT'S A WONDER THAT NO ONE WAS HURT!

MADAM, I DO APOLOGIZE FOR MY WEAK ATTEMPT AT LEVITY DURING THIS STRESSFUL TIME.
AS CURATOR OF THIS MUSEUM, I AM ALWAYS CONCERNED ABOUT OUR COLLECTIONS, BUT NEVER MORE THAN OUR PATRONS, I ASSURE YOU.

WELL, I DIDN'T MEAN TO IMPLY... IT'S JUST THAT THE CHILDREN WERE SO UPSET AND...
YES, YES, I QUITE UNDERSTAND, GOOD LADY. FROM A CURSORY INSPECTION, IT LOOKS AS IF THE DAMAGE IS MINIMAL.

I WOULD HOWEVER, LIKE TO HAVE A BRIEF CHAT WITH THE BOTH OF YOU IN MY OFFICES.
IN THE MEANTIME, I'LL MAKE SURE THAT WE TIDY UP THIS ROOM BEFORE OUR NEXT TOUR GROUP ARRIVES.

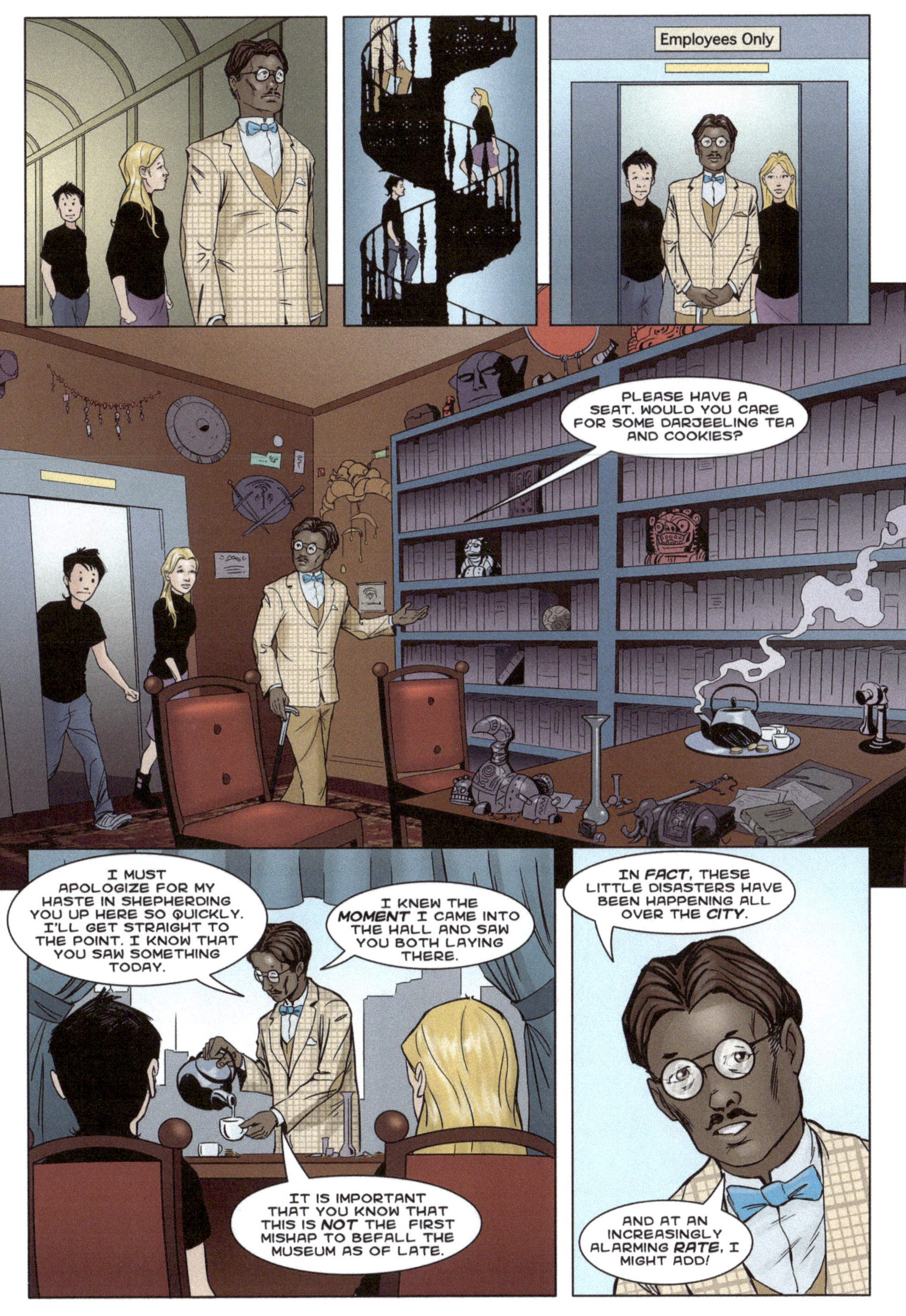
Employees Only
PLEASE HAVE A SEAT. WOULD YOU CARE FOR SOME DARJEELING TEA AND COOKIES?
I MUST APOLOGIZE FOR MY HASTE IN SHEPHERDING YOU UP HERE SO QUICKLY. I'LL GET STRAIGHT TO THE POINT. I KNOW THAT YOU SAW SOMETHING TODAY.
I KNEW THE MOMENT I CAME INTO THE HALL AND SAW YOU BOTH LAYING THERE.
IT IS IMPORTANT THAT YOU KNOW THAT THIS IS NOT THE FIRST MISHAP TO BEFALL THE MUSEUM AS OF LATE.
IN FACT, THESE LITTLE DISASTERS HAVE BEEN HAPPENING ALL OVER THE CITY.
AND AT AN INCREASINGLY ALARMING RATE, I MIGHT ADD!

WELL DR. BEELE, I CAN TELL YOU WHAT I SAW.
I CAME INTO THE HALL AFTER ELLY. BEFORE I PASSED OUT, I CAUGHT A GLIMPSE OF A WEIRD LITTLE MAN.
I THINK HE WAS THE ONE WHO KNOCKED DOWN ALL OF THE ARMOR.
I KNOW THAT YOU TWO HAD NOTHING TO DO WITH THE DAMAGE TO OUR COLLECTION.
I AM MORE CURIOUS AS TO WHAT YOU THINK YOU SAW.
I'LL TELL YOU WHAT I SAW: A GROSS-LOOKING LITTLE RED CREATURE SHOVING ARMOR AROUND LIKE A GIANT GAME OF DOMINOES.
HE WAS LAUGHING AND DANCING AROUND THE WHOLE TIME!
YEAH! HE HAD THIS CRAZY LAUGH LIKE A MIX BETWEEN A CAT, A HYENA AND A SNAKE.
PRETTY CREEPY IF YOU ASK ME.
BUT THAT WAS NOT THE STRANGEST THING...
HE SAW US. HE KNEW WE WERE THERE. AND WHEN HE LOOKED AT ME, IT WAS LIKE I WAS FROZEN RIGHT WHERE I STOOD!
THE WORST PART WAS THE SICK FEELING I HAD THE WHOLE TIME, LIKE HE WAS TAPPING INTO ALL THE BAD THOUGHTS AND FEELINGS WE HAD EVER HAD...
AND BRINGING THEM TO THE SURFACE.
TOM, ELLY, THERE ARE SOME THINGS YOU NEED TO KNOW ABOUT WHAT YOU SAW TODAY.
SIMPLY PUT, YOU HAVE JUST EXPERIENCED A RUN-IN...
...WITH THE NAIN ROUGE!

WHAT? WHO?
I'M SORRY DR. BEELE, BUT WHAT IS A NAIN ROUGE?
IT MEANS "RED DWARF" IN FRENCH. HE IS THE RED DWARF OF DETROIT.
OK, SO WHAT'S A RED DWARF?
DON'T TELL ME WE WERE ATTACKED BY ONE OF SNOW WHITE'S REJECTS!
THIS IS NOTHING TO JOKE ABOUT!
THE NAIN ROUGE IS QUITE REAL AND QUITE DANGEROUS. HE'S AS OLD AS THE CITY ITSELF, MAYBE OLDER.
LEGEND TELLS OF A CREATURE WHOSE APPEARANCE FORESHADOWS TERRIBLE EVENTS WITHIN THE CITY.

HE IS SAID TO HAVE BEEN ATTACKED IN 1701 BY THE FIRST WHITE SETTLER OF DETROIT, ANTOINE DE LA MOTHE CADILLAC.
CADILLAC THREW HIM OUT OF THE FORT PONTCHARTRAIN SETTLEMENT.
EVER SINCE, LUTIN HAS APPEARED IN DETROIT AS A HARBINGER OF DOOM... JUST BEFORE AN IMPENDING DISASTER.

DOCTOR, WHY DID YOU CALL HIM LUTIN?
DID I?

YOU SURE DID.

Le Prince Lutin

HMMM....

CLUNK!
Honi Soit Qui
Mal Y Pense

WHAT'S THIS, DOC?

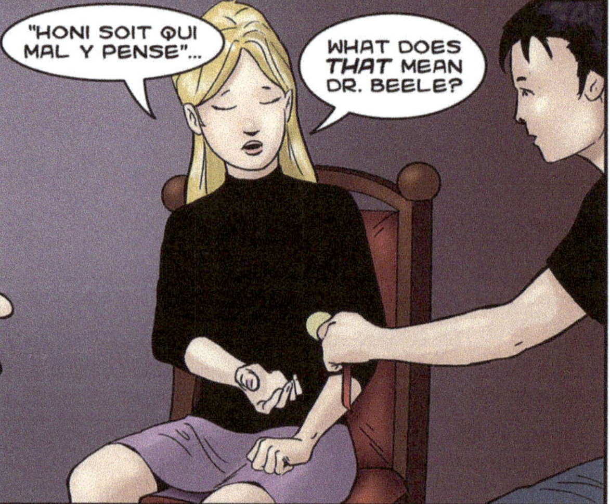

"HONI SOIT QUI MAL Y PENSE"...
WHAT DOES THAT MEAN DR. BEELE?

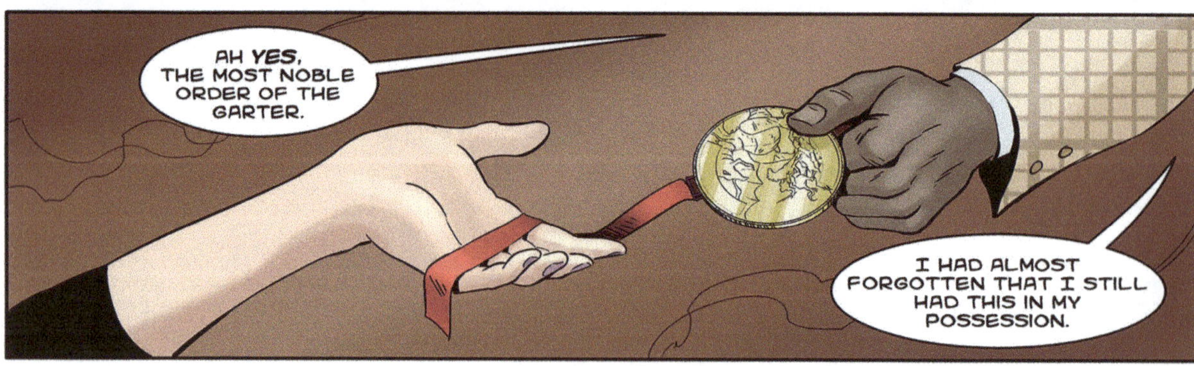

AH YES, THE MOST NOBLE ORDER OF THE GARTER.
I HAD ALMOST FORGOTTEN THAT I STILL HAD THIS IN MY POSSESSION.

THIS MEDALLION WAS GIVEN TO ME BY A VERY SPECIAL FRIEND BACK WHEN I WAS IN ENGLAND.
THE KNIGHT ON THE MEDALLION IS ST. GEORGE, THE PATRON SAINT OF ENGLAND...
FAMOUS FOR SLAYING AN EVIL DRAGON.
THE ORDER IS NOTHING MORE THAN A CHIVALROUS CLUB OF SORTS.
AS FOR THE SAYING, "HONI SOIT QUI MAL Y PENSE", IT IS THE MOTTO OF THIS ORDER IN ARCHAIC FRENCH: "EVIL BE TO THOSE WHO EVIL THINKS".
Honi Soit Qui
Mal Y Pense
...IT WILL EVENTUALLY COME BACK TO YOU IN SOME WAY, SHAPE OR FORM".
SO, ARE YOU A KNIGHT THEN?
A KNIGHT?
WELL, I GUESS IN A WAY I AM.
IN MORE MODERN AMERICAN ENGLISH, ONE MIGHT SAY "IF YOU HAVE EVIL IN YOUR HEART AND MIND...

BUT THAT IS NEITHER HERE NOR THERE, CHILDREN.
I FIND IT PECULIAR THAT YOU WOULD FIND THIS ARTIFACT AT THIS POINT. WE DO HAVE MORE PRESSING MATTERS TO DISCUSS.

SO, FOR NOW, LET'S SET THIS TOPIC ASIDE AND RETURN TO THE ISSUES AT HAND.

"You are invisible when you like it; you cross in one moment the vast space of the universe; you rise without having wings; you go through the ground without dying; you penetrate the abysses of the sea without drowning; you enter everywhere, though the windows and the doors are closed; and, when you decide to, you can let yourself be seen in your natural form."
THERE ARE MANY THINGS THAT I KNOW. HOWEVER, THERE ARE EVEN MORE THINGS OF WHICH I KNOW NOTHING.
Le Prince
THIS BOOK IS A FRENCH FAIRY TALE, DATING BACK TO 1697. I DISCOVERED THIS BOOK DURING AN INTERNSHIP AT THE LOUVRE IN PARIS.
Livres Ancien
SOMETHING DREW ME TO A SMALL BOOK SHOP OUTSIDE OF THE CITY, AND INEXORABLY, TO THIS BOOK.
NOW THINGS ARE BEING REVEALED THAT HAVE BEEN HIDDEN FOR SUCH A VERY LONG TIME, WHICH ONLY CREATES MORE QUESTIONS FOR US ALL.
WHAT I DO KNOW IS THAT "LUTIN" IS FRENCH FOR A MISCHIEVOUS HOBGOBLIN OR HOUSE SPIRIT.
HOWEVER, THE LITTLE CREATURE YOU RAN INTO SEEMS TO BE LUTIN HIMSELF – HE HAS SAID SO. AND HE IS NOT MISCHIEVOUS...
HE IS EVIL.
GEEZ DOC, EVERY TIME WE ASK YOU A QUESTION, THE ANSWERS GET WORSE AND WORSE!
WHAT DO YOU MEAN HE SAID SO?
REMEMBER THAT HORRIBLE HISSING, CRYING SOUND YOU HEARD JUST BEFORE YOU PASSED OUT? WELL, THAT WAS LUTIN CALLING OUT HIS OWN NAME.
HE WANTED YOU BOTH TO HEAR IT.
BUT WHY US, DR. BEELE?
BECAUSE MY DEAR, YOU HAVE BEEN CHOSEN.
THE NAIN ROUGE'S CRY IS HEARD ONLY BY THOSE TO WHICH IT IS INTENDED. FOR MANY ARE CALLED BUT FEW ARE CHOSEN.

DR. BEELE'S WORDS WAFTED THROUGH THEIR EARS, ENCIRCLING THEIR THOUGHTS LIKE THE HEAVY PERFUMED SMOKE OF AN OVERPACKED HOOKAH PIPE.
BEFORE THEY KNEW IT, ELLY AND TOM WERE BACK WITH THEIR GROUP FROM ROYAL OAK MIDDLE SCHOOL, HEADING FOR THE BUS THAT WOULD TAKE THEM BACK NORTH, OUT OF THE CITY

WOW...
YEAH, WOW.

DETOUR

HMM, WE'VE NEVER BEEN THIS WAY HOME BEFORE.

THEY COULD SEE THE DETROIT MOUNTED POLICE STATION ROLLSLOWLY PAST THE SIDE OF THE BUS.
THAT FAMILIAR SMELL OF HAY, LEATHER AND MANURE SEEMED OUT OF PLACE IN THIS URBAN ENVIRONMENT.

TOM, DO YOU SEE THAT?

I SEE IT, I SEE IT!

ELLY AND TOM WERE FROZEN IN FEAR AND FASCINATION. THE HORSE WAS SMILING AT THEM; AN EVIL GRIN.

THEY HAD SEEN THOSE EYES BEFORE, AND THAT GRIN TOO. IT WAS LUTIN.

HE WAS WATCHING THEM AND THEY COULD FEEL IT WITHIN EVERY MUSCLE, EVERY BONE, EVERY SINEW OF THEIR BODIES.
SCHOOL BUS
STOP

WHY US?

ELLY AND TOM HAD GROWN UP TOGETHER IN THE MID-SIZED SUBURB OF ROYAL OAK, WHERE THEY HAD MET IN KINDERGARTEN. ROYAL OAK WAS INCORPORATED AS A CITY IN 1921, BUT ITS NAME WAS MUCH OLDER.

BACK IN 1819, GOVERNOR LEWIS CASS AND SEVERAL COMPANIONS SET OUT ON AN EXPLORATION TO DISPROVE CLAIMS THAT THE MICHIGAN TERRITORY WAS SWAMPY AND UNINHABITABLE.

THEY ENCOUNTERED A STATELY OAK TREE WITH A TRUNK CONSIDERABLY WIDER THAN MOST OAKS.
ITS LARGE BRANCHES REMINDED CASS OF THE LEGEND OF THE ROYAL OAK TREE IN ENGLAND. CASS CHRISTENED THE TREE THE "ROYAL OAK", AND SO THE CITY RECEIVED ITS NAME.

THE ORIGINAL "ROYAL OAK" TREE WAS DESTROYED BY A STRANGE, UNEXPECTED STORM...
...THAT CAME UP FROM THE SOUTH, FROM DETROIT ACTUALLY, MANY YEARS AGO.

NOW, ROYAL OAK WAS THE KIND OF PLACE WHERE PEOPLE LOVED TO LIVE.
IT SEEMED TO LIFT YOU JUST OUT OF REACH OF THE BIG CITY PROBLEMS.

YET, WHENEVER ANYTHING BAD HAPPENED IN DETROIT...
...ITS EFFECTS STILL REVERBERATED OUT AND UP TO ROYAL OAK, WHERE THE CITIZENS WERE THANKFUL THAT THE GROWING PROBLEMS WERE NOT THEIRS...
...AND UNEASY THAT THE NEGATIVE VIBRATIONS WERE COMING NORTH, WITH INCREASING STRENGTH AND FREQUENCY.

ELLY WILLIAMS HAD ALWAYS BEEN ABOVE AVERAGE. IN FACT, ONE MIGHT CALL HER AN *OVERACHIEVER* — IN *EVERYTHING*. BUT, DESPITE HER ACHIEVEMENTS, ELLY OFTEN APPEARED SHY AND SLIGHTLY HESITANT. IT WAS AS IF SHE WAS BEING CHASED BY THE SHADOW OF HER TRUE SELF, HIDING BEHIND THE ACTIVITY UNTIL THE DARK SHADE PASSED BY HER UNNOTICED.
TOM WAS NOT MUCH OF A TALKER, HE WAS MORE OF A DOER. TOM WAS NEVER IMPRESSED WITH ALL OF ELLY'S MEDALS, CERTIFICATES OR AWARDS OR ANY OF THAT STUFF. HE WAS CONFIDENT IN HIMSELF.
THE AWARDS AND ACCOLADES BECAME A SMOKE SCREEN TO CAMOUFLAGE THE FEAR AND DOUBT THAT WAS JUST BELOW THE SURFACE OF HER THINLY VEILED ANXIETY.
IF THEY HAD *AWARDS* FOR BAD JUDGMENT, TOM WOULD HAVE MORE TROPHIES THAN ELLY.
Try harder!
TOM DEMINE WAS AWARE OF ALL THIS. WELL, ACTUALLY, HE NEVER REALLY THOUGHT *TOO* MUCH ABOUT ELLY'S "EMOTIONS". HE JUST KNEW ELLY, INSIDE AND OUT.
TOM WAS A SCATTERBRAINED FREE SPIRIT WHO WAS KNOWN TO LEAP BEFORE HE EVER THOUGHT TO LOOK. OH, HE NEVER DID ANYTHING *REALLY* BAD, JUST LITTLE THINGS: ROLLING SMOKE BOMBS DOWN THE HALL IN SCHOOL, MISSING CLASS ASSIGNMENTS, OR FORGETTING TO SHUT THE WATER OFF WHEN FILLING THE SWIMMING POOL.
AS THE PAIR MOVED INTO MIDDLE SCHOOL, THEY BOTH LEARNED TO KEEP THEIR SPECIAL RELATIONSHIP UNDER WRAPS.
TOM HAD THE CONFIDENCE THAT ELLY WAS LACKING, WHILE ELLY HAD THE DISCIPLINE TO GET THINGS DONE. THEY COULD COMMUNICATE *INSTINCTIVELY*, OFTEN WITHOUT SPEAKING, OPEN AND FREELY.
A FEW KIDS MADE COMMENTS ABOUT THEM BEING "LOVEBIRDS" OR A "CUTE COUPLE", SO THEY WERE ALWAYS CAREFUL HOW MUCH TIME THEY SPENT TOGETHER.
DURING THIS TIME OF CONFUSION AND MYSTERY, THEY BOTH FELT THAT IF SOMETHING BAD WAS GOING TO HAPPEN IT WOULD BE BETTER IF IT HAPPENED TO THEM BOTH — TOGETHER. AFTER ALL, MISERY DOES LOVE COMPANY.

Computer Lab
TOM TOLD ELLY TO MEET HIM AFTER SCHOOL IN THE MEDIA CENTER, SO THAT THEY COULD FIGURE OUT WHAT WAS REALLY GOING ON. ON *MOST* DAYS, THE CENTER WAS OPEN FOR A FEW HOURS AFTER SCHOOL.

ELLY, GET *IN* HERE, YOU'VE GOT TO SEE THIS!

I THOUGHT WE WERE GOING TO *TALK*, NOT PLAY GAMES ON THE COMPUTER.
I'M NOT PLAYING *GAMES*, I'M DOING RESEARCH ON THE NAIN ROUGE, AND LOOK WHAT I FOUND!

REMEMBER, DR. BEELE SAID THAT THE LITTLE *MONSTER* WAS THROWN OUT OF FORT PONTCHARTRAIN OVER 300 YEARS AGO.
BIG DEAL, WE ALREADY *KNEW* THAT.

YEAH, BUT DID YOU KNOW THAT FORT PONTCHARTRAIN WAS *ALSO* KNOWN AS FORT DETROIT, WHICH IS WHERE THE CITY ACTUALLY STARTED?
OK, YOU'VE GOT MY ATTENTION.
WHAT *ELSE*?

HERE. REMEMBER WHEN WE DID THAT *GENEALOGY* PROJECT LAST YEAR?
AND WE FOUND OUT THAT WE WERE RELATED WAY, WAY BACK, GENERATIONS AGO?

HOW COULD I FORGET THE "KISSING COUSINS" NICKNAME EVERYONE SLAPPED ON US?

GET OVER IT EL, I DID!
ANYWAY, DO YOU REMEMBER WHO OUR COMMON ANCESTOR WAS? MARIANNE DE TONTY!

SO WHAT OF IT? I DON'T EVEN KNOW WHO THAT *IS*.
HERE, READ *THIS*!
Pierre Alphonse de Tonty was born in 1659 to Laurent and Angelique (de Liette) de Tonty. Some time after 1689 and before 1701, Tonty married Marianne la Marque, daughter of Francois la Marque. This was Marianne's third marriage.
Tonty was the Captain of Cadillac's party, which founded Fort Pontchartrain du Detroit in 1701. He was a loyal, trusted officer. He was known to the Native Americans as "the man with the iron hand" due to an artificial limb.
OK, I *GET* IT. WE'RE RELATED TO MARIANNE DE TONTY, SO WHAT'S THE BIG DEAL?

THE BIG DEAL IS THAT HER HUSBAND WAS AN OFFICER IN CADILLAC'S EXPEDITION. HE HELPED FOUND FORT PONTCHARTRAIN!

HMMMMM...

I BET THAT'S WHY WE WERE CHOSEN. SOMETHING MUST HAVE HAPPENED WITH THE NAIN ROUGE BACK THEN AND SINCE WE ARE RELATED TO THESE FIRST SETTLERS, WE HAVE TO PAY THE PRICE!
THE GRAVITY OF THIS MOMENT SOON SETTLED ON BOTH ELLY AND TOM. FOR THE FIRST TIME, THEY REALIZED THERE WAS MUCH MORE GOING ON AROUND THEM THAN WHAT APPEARED TO THE NAKED EYE.

IT WAS AS IF AN INVISIBLE STORM WAS BEGINNING TO SWIRL AROUND THEM, CREATING A GROWING VORTEX OF ENERGY, INFORMATION AND STRANGE HISTORY.

THEY KNEW SOMETHING WAS NOT RIGHT AND THEY WERE THE ONES WHO WERE GOING TO HAVE TO FIX IT.

WE NEED TO FIND A WAY TO CONTACT DR. BEELE. HE'S THE ONE PERSON WHO CAN HELP US.

ROYAL OAK
YEAH, BUT HOW ARE WE GOING TO GET ALL THE WAY BACK DOWN TO DETROIT WITHOUT SOMEONE ASKING US A BUNCH OF QUESTIONS?

WELL, WE'LL JUST HAVE TO FIND A WAY. WE CAN'T AFFORD TO WAIT TOO LONG.

I'M JUST AFRAID THAT SOMETHING ELSE BAD WILL HAPPEN IF WE DON'T DO SOMETHING RIGHT NOW!
UM... WELL...
I COULD STEAL THE PRINCIPAL'S CAR AND WE COULD TOTALLY DRIVE DOWN THERE RIGHT NOW, IF YOU WANT.

OK EL, GEEZ, I WAS JUST KIDDING, LIGHTEN UP...
LET'S SEE IF OUR PARENTS WILL GIVE US A RIDE DOWNTOWN THIS WEEKEND.
WE CAN TELL THEM WE HAVE TO DO RESEARCH FOR A TERM PAPER OR SOMETHING.
WELL, NOW YOU'RE BACK ON TRACK!
THAT SOUNDS LIKE AN IDEA WE CAN MAKE HAPPEN. I'LL WORK ON MY MOM AND DAD TONIGHT.

GREAT! I'LL SEE WHAT I CAN DO WHEN I GET HOME.
AWESOME, THIS COULD BE THE BIG CLUE WE HAVE ALL BEEN LOOKING FOR.
I'M SURE THAT DR. BEELE WILL BE ANXIOUS TO LEARN WHAT WE'VE DISCOVERED.

THE NEXT TWO DAYS PASSED IN A FOG OF MUNDANE REPETITION. ELLY AND TOM WENT THROUGH THEIR DAILY ROUTINES WITH ROBOTIC *PRECISION*, NOT WANTING TO LET ANYONE KNOW WHAT THEY HAD LEARNED.
INSIDE, THEIR MINDS WERE *RACING* WITH RAPID CONJECTURE AND ANTICIPATION, WONDERING WHAT WAS NEXT.

I THOUGHT FRIDAY WOULD *NEVER* GET HERE!

HONEY, CAN WE *TALK* TO YOU FOR A MINUTE?

SURE MOM, JUST A MINUTE!

SWEETIE, I GOT SOME BAD NEWS FROM *WORK* TODAY...

DAD, DON'T WORRY. WHATEVER IT IS, I CAN *TAKE* IT, REALLY...

WELL, I JUST LET YOUR MOM KNOW THAT I WAS LET GO FROM MY JOB. WE THOUGHT *YOU* SHOULD KNOW TOO. THIS WAS MY LAST WEEK.

THEY SAID THAT I CAN COME BACK AND CLEAN MY DESK OUT ON SATURDAY.
I GUESS THEY WANT TO SAVE ME THE EMBARRASSMENT OF HAVING TO FACE EVERYONE AT THE OFFICE.

AT LEAST THEY LEFT ME *SOME* DIGNITY, I GUESS.

A *LOT* OF PEOPLE ARE GETTING LAID OFF. NOT JUST FROM *MY* BUSINESS BUT ALL AROUND THE AREA.
NOW I GUESS WE'RE EXPERIENCING THAT FIRST HAND.

TOM, IT'S ME. I GOT SOME SAD NEWS. MY DAD WAS LAID OFF FROM HIS JOB AT COMPUWARE.
THAT'S AWFUL. I CAN REALLY UNDERSTAND, SINCE MY MOM WAS LET GO FROM GM JUST LAST MONTH.
THE ONLY GOOD THING IS THAT NOW WE CAN GET A RIDE INTO TOWN TOMORROW WITH MY DAD, WHILE HE SETTLES HIS AFFAIRS AT THE OFFICE.

THE CLOUDS SEEMED TO HANG A BIT LOWER AS THEY APPROACHED EIGHT MILE ROAD, THE CITY LIMITS.

TOM, DO YOU SMELL SOMETHING?

LIKE BURNT ASHES...
...OR BRIMSTONE?

I THINK I'M GOING TO BE SICK...!
DON'T! THAT'S JUST WHAT HE WANTS. HE'S TRYING TO STOP US FROM GETTING ANY FARTHER.

OK KIDS, I'LL SEE YOU IN A FEW HOURS. I'LL PICK YOU UP RIGHT HERE.
CALL ME ON MY CELL IF YOU HAVE ANY PROBLEMS.

THE DETROIT INSTIT...
I WONDER WHAT HE'S THINKING ABOUT.

HE SEEMS... TROUBLED SOMEHOW. CONFUSED.

THE DETRO...
THE THINKER

THE DETRO...
ELLY...? DO YOU SEE THAT?
THE THINKER
THE DETRO...
THE THINKER

CHAPTER 2

TOM CAME RUNNING IN AND CAUGHT UP WITH ELLY JUST IN TIME TO SEE...

CITED LITTLE
E DANCING AND
ABOUT IN A
D FRENZY OF
ND JOY.

JUST AS ELLY AN
TAKING IN THE EN

...THE LITTLE MAN STOPPED. THE DANCING STOPPED. THE ODD, QUEER CATERWAULING SOUND HE MADE STOPPED.

CREEEAK!
IS THAT...?
LUTIN!
EEEEEEEAAAAASSSSSSSSSSSSSSSSSSSSSGGGGGG!!!
RUN!!

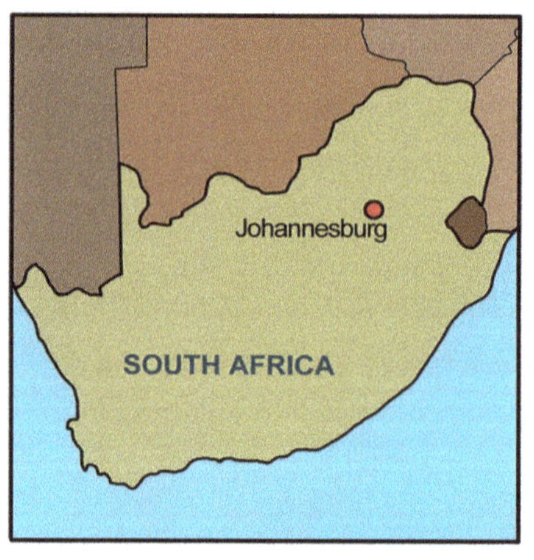

HIERONYMUS STANLEY BEELE WAS BORN IN JOHANNESBURG, SOUTH AFRICA, TO AMERICAN MISSIONARY PARENTS. FOR THE FIRST FEW WEEKS OF HIS LIFE HE RELAXED QUIETLY IN A MODEST CLAY-BRICK HOME JUST ABOVE THE BUSTLING CITY.

HE HAS BEEN TRAVELLING AND ADVENTURING EVER SINCE, ATTENDING VARIOUS SCHOOLS AROUND THE WORLD. HE MADE FRIENDS EASILY AND ASSIMILATED QUICKLY INTO MYRIAD CULTURES. HE HAD MORE ADVENTURES AS A BOY THAN *MOST* PEOPLE HAVE IN A LIFETIME.

HE HAD ZIP-LINED THROUGH THE COSTA RICAN RAINFOREST, CLIMBED THE ACROPOLIS OF ATHENS, AND SET UP BASE CAMP AT THE FOOT OF MT. EVEREST, ALL BEFORE THE RIPE OLD AGE OF SIXTEEN.

HE OFTEN FOUND HIMSELF WALKING DOWN HIGH STREET ALONE, HEADING TOWARD HIS BLAND, GRAY UPPER FLAT. IT WAS NOT UNTIL HE RETURNED TO HIS HOMELAND IN THE UNITED STATES THAT HE BEGAN TO CONNECT WITH *PEOPLE* INSTEAD OF *PLACES*. HE INTERNED AT THE METROPOLITAN MUSEUM OF ART IN NEW YORK CITY.

EVENTUALLY HE COMPLETED HIS EDUCATION AND BECAME *DR.* BEELE, HIS INTERNSHIPS GROWING INTO FULL-TIME POSITIONS. HE MOVED AROUND THE U.S., TAKING VARIOUS POSITIONS ALL OVER THE COUNTRY, AND FINALLY ARRIVED IN DETROIT.

AS CURATOR OF THE DETROIT INSTITUTE OF ARTS, HE AT LAST FOUND TRUE HAPPINESS AND HARMONY.

HIS ROLE ALLOWED HIM TO MAINTAIN CLOSE CONTACT WITH THE PUBLIC, WHILE STILL BEING ABLE TO FOCUS ON HIS LOVE OF ART.

WHEN THE STRANGE HAPPENINGS BEGAN IN THE MUSEUM, DR. BEELE STARTED TO SEE THAT HE HAD SIGNED UP FOR MORE THAN HE ORIGINALLY *BARGAINED* FOR!

HE THOUGHT THE COMMOTION MIGHT JUST GO AWAY ON ITS OWN, BUT THE NAIN ROUGE WAS GETTING STRONGER. AND *NOW* THERE WERE *CHILDREN* INVOLVED! IN ALL OF HIS TRAVELS AND ADVENTURES, HE HAD *NEVER* FELT AS MUCH ANXIETY AS HE FELT NOW. THIS SITUATION WAS NO LONGER JUST ABOUT HIM AND HIS MUSEUM.

IT WAS ABOUT THE LIVES OF TWO YOUNG PEOPLE, THE CITY, THE SURROUNDING REGION AND *ALL* OF ITS INHABITANTS.

AS THE GRAVITY AND WEIGHT OF THE WORLD SETTLED DOWN UPON HIS SHOULDERS, FOR THE FIRST TIME IN HIS LIFE, DR. BEELE DID NOT KNOW WHAT HE WAS GOING TO DO NEXT.

DID YOU SEE THAT?!
IF YOU ARE ASKING WHETHER I SAW YOU AND ELLY BLOW THROUGH MY MUSEUM DOORS LIKE A ROGUE TORNADO, THEN THE ANSWER IS YES, I DID SEE THAT.
NO! DID YOU SEE THE STATUE? THE NAIN ROUGE!
IT'S AFTER US!
HMMMMM...

WELL?

COME WITH ME!

THE OFFICE SEEMED LESS INTIMIDATING THAN BEFORE, AND THEY WERE HAPPY TO SEE THAT THE COOKIES AND TEA HAD BEEN REFRESHED SINCE THEIR LAST VISIT.

DOCTOR, YOU WOULDN'T BELIEVE THE THINGS WE'VE SEEN SINCE WE TALKED THE LAST TIME.
IT'S AS IF THE NAIN ROUGE IS FOLLOWING US. LIKE HE WANTS SOMETHING FROM US!

REMEMBER I TOLD YOU WHEN WE FIRST MET THAT THERE ARE MANY THINGS I KNOW AND MANY MORE THINGS ABOUT WHICH I KNOW NOTHING?
WELL, LUTIN IS ONE CREATURE THAT FALLS DEEPER INTO MY "NOT-KNOWING" CATEGORY.

WELL, THERE ARE A FEW THINGS ELLY AND I CAN SHARE WITH YOU THAT MAY HELP. LAST YEAR, WE BOTH LEARNED THAT WE WERE RELATED TO MARIANNE DE TONTY.
WE JUST FOUND OUT THIS WEEK THAT SHE WAS MARRIED TO ONE OF THE CAPTAINS AT FORT PONTCHARTRAIN.

HOW DID YOU KNOW THAT? WE READ ON THE INTERNET THAT THE NATIVE AMERICANS CALLED HER HUSBAND PIERRE THAT.
IS THAT SO? VERY INTERESTING INDEED. SHE WAS MARRIED TO THE MAN WITH THE IRON HAND...

YES, HE HAD AN ARTIFICIAL HAND. AND DO YOU KNOW HOW HE LOST IT?
NO.

WELL, SAD TO SAY, IT WAS LUTIN.

IT SEEMS THAT DURING THE FOUNDING OF FORT PONTCHARTRAIN, CADILLAC HAD MADE A DEAL WITH THE NATIVE AMERICANS TO SETTLE TRACTS OF *LAND* NEAR THE RIVER.
THE NATIVES WARNED CADILLAC ABOUT THE NAIN ROUGE. THEY TOLD HIM THAT THIS CREATURE WAS PART OF THE LAND AND NEEDED TO BE *APPEASED* IN ORDER THAT THE SETTLERS MIGHT WORK AND FARM THE LAND IN PEACE.
CADILLAC BRUSHED AWAY THEIR WARNINGS AS SILLY, PRIMITIVE SUPERSTITIONS AND ALLOWED HIS PEOPLE TO BEGIN BUILDING HOUSES, PLOWING FIELDS, AND PLANTING CROPS.
AFTER A SHORT WHILE, THE SETTLERS BEGAN TO NOTICE THAT SOME OF THEIR LIVESTOCK WAS *MISSING*. THEN, *CROPS* BEGAN TO DRY UP AND WITHER.
IN SHORT, THE SETTLEMENT WAS *FAILING*.
ONE EVENING, WHEN CADILLAC AND SOME OF HIS OFFICERS WERE IN THEIR CABIN...
...THEY HEARD A MOURNFUL, TERRIBLE *CRY* OUTSIDE THEIR DOOR.

UPON OPENING THE DOOR, THEY LOOKED DOWN UPON A SMALL, LITTLE MAN, NO HIGHER THAN A YARD STICK.
THE TINY STRANGER STEPPED INSIDE THE CABIN AND INTRODUCED HIMSELF AS "LUTIN: THE STEWARD OF THE STRAITS." LUTIN WAS VERY CORDIAL AND FRIENDLY.
HE MADE IT CLEAR THAT HE WANTED TO WORK WITH THE SETTLERS TO BUILD A GREAT CITY UPON HIS SPOT IN THE WILDERNESS. HE WAS WILLING TO SHARE HIS KNOWLEDGE OF THE LAND, AND EVERYTHING AROUND THEM.
THINGS TURNED UGLY. CADILLAC AND HIS MEN LAUGHED AT THE LITTLE MAN. THEY MOCKED HIM AND CALLED HIM A FOOL. THEY STATED QUITE CLEARLY THAT THEY WOULD TAKE WHATEVER THEY WANTED, WHENEVER THEY WANTED, FROM WHOMEVER THEY WANTED.

ONE OF CADILLAC'S OFFICERS, PIERRE DE TONTY, REACHED OUT TO SUBDUE THE CREATURE...
AT THIS, THE SLIGHT STRANGER BEGAN HOPPING AND JUMPING UP AND DOWN. HIS SKIN TURNED AN ANGRY, HOT RED. HIS FINGERNAILS MANIFESTED INTO CLAWS AND HIS FACE GNARLED UP INTO CONTORTED KNOTS.
...AND WAS BITTEN MOST FIERCELY UPON HIS LEFT HAND.
A GREAT COMMOTION ENSUED AND LUTIN ESCAPED, BUT BEFORE HE DID, HE HISSED OUT THESE PARTING WORDS:
"KEEP WHAT YOU STEAL AND STEAL WHAT YOU KEEP
THE SHEPHERD MUST PAY FOR HIS SINS WITH HIS SHEEP."
NOW, EVER SINCE THAT FATEFUL NIGHT, LUTIN HAS APPEARED JUST BEFORE ANY DISASTER BEFALLS THE CITY OF DETROIT.

IT ALL MAKES SENSE NOW. THE STORY GOES ON TO SAY...

...THAT PIERRE DE TONTY LOST HIS MANGLED HAND AFTER THE BITE THE NAIN ROUGE HAD GIVEN HIM BECAME INFECTED.
THE CURSE THAT LUTIN UTTERED BEFORE HE DISAPPEARED HAS BEEN CAST ON BOTH YOUR FAMILIES.

I AM AFRAID TO TELL YOU, THAT YOU TWO ARE THE SHEEP THAT LUTIN WAS TALKING ABOUT.
THIS CURSE IS YOUR LEGACY.

RIIIING!

HI DAD ...OK, THANKS.

D–DR. BEELE? WHAT DOES ALL THIS MEAN FOR US? I MEAN, FOR ELLY AND ME?
IT'S MY DAD. HE WANTS US TO WALK OVER TO HIS OFFICE. HE'S GONNA BE TIED UP FOR AN HOUR AND WANTS US TO MEET HIM AT THE HARD ROCK CAFE FOR LUNCH.

THIS I DO KNOW; YOU ARE THE HEIRS TO STOLEN LAND; THE LAND UPON WHICH THIS ENTIRE CITY WAS BUILT.
LUTIN SEEMS TO BELIEVE THAT THERE IS A DEBT THAT REMAINS UNPAID AND YOU TWO ARE THE DEBTORS.

NOW, THAT EXPLAINS THE "WHY YOU" QUESTION. BUT WHAT I FAIL TO UNDERSTAND IS THE "WHY NOW" QUESTION.
WHY WOULD LUTIN WANT TO CALL IN HIS MARKER NOW?

IT WAS CLEAR THAT LIFE IN DETROIT WAS GETTING PROGRESSIVELY WORSE. ECONOMIC WOES, PEOPLE LOSING JOBS, POLITICAL CORRUPTION, AND A PROFESSIONAL FOOTBALL TEAM THAT HAD NOT WON A CHAMPIONSHIP SINCE 1957!
SO *HOW* ARE WE SUPPOSED TO PAY BACK A DEBT THAT SOME DISTANT RELATIVES OWED 300 *YEARS* AGO?

THAT, I'M AFRAID, YOU WILL HAVE TO ASK LUTIN *HIMSELF*.

AND HOW ARE WE SUPPOSED TO FIND HIM? HE SEEMS TO BE *EVERYWHERE* AND *NOWHERE*?

I SUSPECT THAT IN HIS OWN GOOD TIME, *HE* WILL FIND *YOU*.

DETROIT INSTITUTE OF ARTS
WITH HEAVY HEARTS AND SPINNING HEADS, THEY THANKED THE CURATOR AND MADE THEIR WAY OUT OF THE MUSEUM.

ELLY AND TOM WERE BOTH ACUTELY AWARE, AND YET UNAWARE OF THE CITY THAT WRAPPED AROUND THEM AS THEY WALKED.
NEITHER KNEW WHETHER OR NOT LUTIN WOULD JUMP OUT AND ATTACK THEM ON THE SPOT. THE ANTICIPATION OF NOT KNOWING WAS KILLING THEM.

THE TWO YOUNG ADULTS WERE FLYING QUICKLY ACROSS INTERSECTIONS, ABANDONED CHURCHES, AND ABANDONED BUILDINGS.
HE WAS THE PREDATOR. THEY WERE THE PREY. THERE WERE TOO MANY PLACES TO HIDE; TOO MANY SHADOWS TO CAMOUFLAGE THE EVIL THEY KNEW WAS WATCHING AND WAITING.

DO YOU FEEL LIKE YOU'RE...
...IN A DREAM. EVERYTHING IS MOVING IN SLOW MOTION.
SOMETHING'S COMING.

1 CAMPUS MARTUS: THE COMPUWARE BUILDING

CAN YOU CALL MY FATHER AND LET HIM KNOW THAT WE'RE IN THE BUILDING?
SURE THING, MISS.

MY DAD SAYS HE'S RUNNING A FEW MINUTES LATE. WE'LL MEET HIM AT THE RESTAURANT IN 20 MINUTES.
WHY DON'T WE BROWSE AROUND A BIT?

WHERE TO?
ROCK
LET'S GO TO THE BOOK STORE!
BOOKS
HEY... DO YOU SMELL THAT?

IF YOU MEAN THAT ROTTEN EGG SMELL, YES, THANKS FOR ASKING.

SNIFF SNIFF
IT WASN'T ME! I KNOW I'VE SMELLED THAT SMELL BEFORE...

WHAT'S THAT?
EEEEEEEAAAAAASSSSSSSSSSSSSSSSSSSSS!!!

GOOD DAY TO YOU.
Hi! I'm LUTIN
HELLO...?
I HAVE BEEN EXPECTING YOU BOTH FOR SOME TIME NOW.
NAIN ROUGE!
MY NAME IS LUTIN. AND YOU ARE IMPERTINENT.
I CERTAINLY KNOW WHO YOU ARE. I ALSO KNOW THAT DR. BEELE HAS SHARED WITH YOU THE LITTLE HE KNOWS ABOUT ME, THE VERY LITTLE, I MUST SAY.

SINCE YOU WILL SOON BE MINE...

... I THINK IT ONLY FAIR THAT YOU KNOW THE COMPLETE TALE OF YOUR UNFORTUNATE FATE.

I AM AS OLD AS THE LAND; AS OLD AS THE RIVER, THE TREES AND EVERYTHING THAT GROWS HERE.

THE NATIVE AMERICANS UNDERSTOOD THIS. THEY RESPECTED ME, HONORED ME. BUT THEN YOUR PEOPLE CAME.

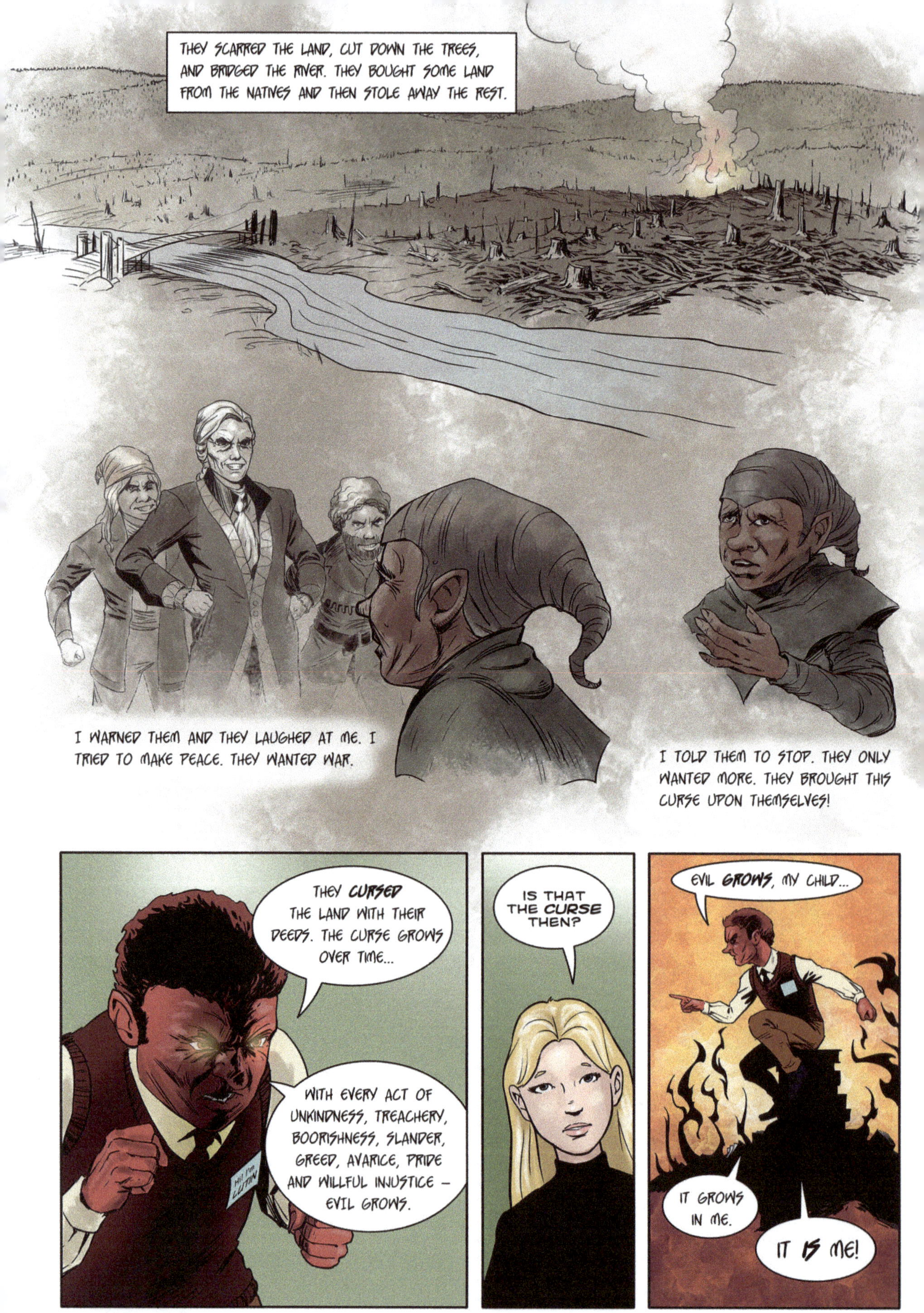

THEY SCARRED THE LAND, CUT DOWN THE TREES, AND BRIDGED THE RIVER. THEY BOUGHT SOME LAND FROM THE NATIVES AND THEN STOLE AWAY THE REST.

I WARNED THEM AND THEY LAUGHED AT ME. I TRIED TO MAKE PEACE. THEY WANTED WAR.

I TOLD THEM TO STOP. THEY ONLY WANTED MORE. THEY BROUGHT THIS CURSE UPON THEMSELVES!

IF YOU REALLY *MUST* KNOW THE ENTIRE STORY, I WILL TELL YOU.
YOUR GOOD *DOCTOR* FRIEND HAS PROBABLY FILLED YOUR HEADS WITH TOO MANY *FALSEHOODS* ALREADY.
NOW, IT IS TIME FOR YOU TO HEAR THE *TRUTH*. IT IS ONLY FAIR AFTER ALL, FOR IT IS *YOUR* STORY AS WELL.
HERE IS YOUR BELOVED *CITY*!
HERE IS WHERE IT ALL *STARTED*, WHEN THE LAND WAS FRESH, NEW AND UNDEFILED.
Hi! I'm LUTIN

NOW, LET US GO INSIDE THE CABIN AND SEE...
...WHAT HOSPITALITY YOUR KIN-FOLK HAVE IN STORE FOR US.
DON'T WORRY, THROUGH MY DARK MAGIC, WE CANNOT BE SEEN OR HEARD, EVEN THOUGH WE CAN SEE AND UNDERSTAND EVERYTHING.
ELLY, IS THAT ANTOINE DE LA MOTHE CADILLAC?
EEEEEEAAAASSSSSSSSSSSSSSSSSSSS!!
YES! AND THAT MIGHT BE PIERRE DE TONTY!

OPEN THE DOOR AND SEE WHAT THAT NOISE IS!
HEY!
I SEEK TO SPEAK TO THE ONE IN CHARGE!
WHO ARE YOU, LITTLE MAN OF THE WOODS...
...TO DEMAND AN AUDIENCE WITH ANYONE?
YOU HAVE COME HERE AND SETTLED THE LANDS FOR WHICH I AM RESPONSIBLE. I COME HERE TO WORK WITH YOU, TO ENSURE THAT ALL OF OUR NEEDS ARE TENDED TO PROPERLY.
THERE IS MUCH I HAVE TO OFFER!

WHY, YOU IMPERTINENT IMP! YOU DARE TO SPEAK TO THE GREAT CADILLAC IN SUCH A MANNER?!!
YOU SPEAK OUT OF TURN AND FAR BEYOND YOUR STATION.
BE GONE FOOL, BEFORE I SQUASH YOU LIKE A BUG UNDER MY BOOT!
SSSSSSSSSSS!!!
THROW HIM OUT!
THUMP!
KRACK!!

SLAM!
CLUNK!
THAT LITTLE BEAST TORE MY HAND TO SHREDS!
KEEEP WHAT YOU SSSSTEAL AND SSSSTEAL WHAT YOU KEEEP
THE SSSSHEPERD MUSSST PAY FOR HIS SSSSINS WITH HIS

HEY!
SOMETHING'S HAPPENING...!

WHAM!
CLUNK!

YOU SEE, I WAS ONCE UPON A TIME THE STEWARD OF THE LAND.

AND NOW FOR CENTURIES I HAVE BEEN THE STEWARD OF THE CURSE!
EACH ACT OF EVIL UPON THIS LAND RESIDES IN ME.
FOR MANY YEARS, THERE WAS A BALANCE OF GOOD AND EVIL IN DETROIT; CONTROLLING MY POWER; DIMINISHING MY PRESENCE.
BUT LATELY, I GROW STRONG. THE ACTS OF HUMANITY HAVE ERRED ON THE SIDE OF WICKEDNESS, FEEDING MY INSATIABLE APPETITE. THIS CURSED LAND HAS BECOME MY GARDEN OF EDEN.

BUT WHY US... WHY RIGHT NOW?

WHY, YOU ARE THE TIPPING POINT MY BOY. THE TIPPING POINT BETWEEN GOOD AND EVIL.
THE POINT WHERE THE GOOD OF THE PEOPLE IS NO LONGER STRONG ENOUGH...
...TO HOLD BACK THE EVIL THAT HAS BEEN BUILDING UP BENEATH THEIR FEET!

AND... WHAT ABOUT US, THEN?

OH YOU. WHY, YOU ARE THE LEGACY, THE RANSOM THAT FULFILLS THE CURSE!

YOUR DEATHS WILL BE MY RISING!

AND NOW I AM SURE YOU LOOK TO RUN AWAY AND HIDE OR MUSTER UP YOUR REMAINING CRUMBS OF COURAGE AND ATTACK ME DIRECTLY.
I ENCOURAGE YOU TO LET GO OF SUCH SILLY SCHEMES.

YOU SEE, IT WILL NOT BE ME WHO ENDS YOUR LIVES; IT WILL BE THE LAND.

WHAT THE HECK IS THAT SUPPOSED TO MEAN? HOW CAN THE LAND KILL US?

MY SILLY BOY, DID I NOT TELL YOU THAT I WAS THE KEEPER OF LAND, THE STEWARD OF THIS REGION?
AS STEWARD, I MUST ADMINISTER TO THE BUSINESS AT HAND.
I AM NO CHEAP KILLER. NO, I AM MERELY THE EXECUTOR OF DEALINGS THAT HAVE ACCRUED FOR CENTURIES.
NOW THE PAYMENT HAS COME DUE.

CHAPTER 3

TOM CAME RUNNING IN AND CAUGHT UP WITH ELLY JUST IN TIME TO SEE...

CITED LITTLE
E DANCING AND
ABOUT IN A
D FRENZY OF
ND JOY.

JUST AS ELLY AN
TAKING IN THE ENT

...THE LITTLE MAN STOPPED. THE DANCING STOPPED. THE ODD, QUEER CATERWAULING SOUND HE MADE STOPPED.

SO, WHEN WILL IT HAPPEN?
TO BE EXACT, MY DEAR: MIDNIGHT ON JULY 24TH.
THE VERY DAY THAT ANTOINE DE LA MOTHE CADILLAC BEGAN THE SETTLEMENT OF DETROIT, OVER 300 YEARS AGO.
WHAT LUTIN TOLD THE CHILDREN WAS TRUE. CADILLAC'S EXPEDITION REACHED THE DETROIT RIVER ON JULY 23, 1701. THEY SET UP CAMP THERE AND SPENT THE NIGHT SOUTH OF WHERE THE CITY LIES TODAY.
IT WAS NOT UNTIL THE FOLLOWING DAY THAT CADILLAC'S PARTY TRAVELED NORTH ON THE DETROIT RIVER LOOKING FOR A PLACE TO BUILD THEIR SETTLEMENT.
IT WAS ALSO AT THAT SPOT WHERE THE NAIN ROUGE FIRST OBSERVED THE STRANGE, PALE CREATURES, LEVELING TREES AND GOUGING INTO THE LAND HE HAD SWORN TO PROTECT.
YES, THAT IS THE DAY THE CURSE FIRST FORMED, AND IT WILL BE THE DAY THAT THE CURSE COMES TO FRUITION...
...AND I WILL RULE THE LAND ONCE MORE!

LUNCH TASTED LIKE ASHES AND SOOT.
ELLY'S DAD DID NOT EVEN NOTICE THE DREARY MOOD OF THE TWO CHILDREN AS THEY ATE WITH LITTLE ZEAL OR INTEREST.

JUST THINK OF THE SITUATION THEY WERE ALL IN: AN UNEMPLOYED FATHER AND TWO CHILDREN WHO KNEW THAT SHORTLY THEY WERE GOING TO DIE. BUT STILL THEY FELT A TWINGE OF HAPPINESS, OF SLIGHT JOY BENEATH THE LOW-HANGING CLOUDS.
A BACK-AND-FORTH CYCLE OF DENIAL, ANGER, BARGAINING, DEPRESSION AND ACCEPTANCE SWIRLED AROUND INSIDE THEIR HEADS, AS THEY TRIED TO COPE WITH THE REALIZATION OF THEIR OWN DEATHS.

WE'RE ABOUT TO BE KILLED BY A RED TROLL JUST BECAUSE SOME DISTANT ANCESTOR STOLE HIS LAND?
IF WE TOLD ANYONE THAT, WE'D BOTH BE IN THERAPY FOR SURE.
YEAH...

...LIFE'S NOT FAIR.

AFTER A WHILE, ELLY AND TOM BECAME DEPRESSED WITH THE EVER-PRESENT THOUGHT THAT THEY WERE DOOMED.
THE SUMMER THAT THEY NORMALLY LOOKED FORWARD TO ALL YEAR LONG HAD BECOME A DARK WAITING ROOM OF DESPAIR.

ELLY AND TOM STILL MADE A FEW TRIPS TO THE BEACH...

GOOD CATCH, TODD!
...SAW A TIGERS BASEBALL GAME...

...AND EVEN WENT TO A COUPLE OF CONCERTS.

BUT THEY COULD NOT HELP RETURNING TO THE THOUGHT THAT THEIR TIME ON THIS EARTH WAS WANING. SOON THEY WOULD BE NO MORE.

WELL, EL, I GUESS THIS IS IT. IN A FEW WEEKS, WE'RE TOAST.

WE AREN'T TOAST YET...
...AND I HAVE A PLAN!

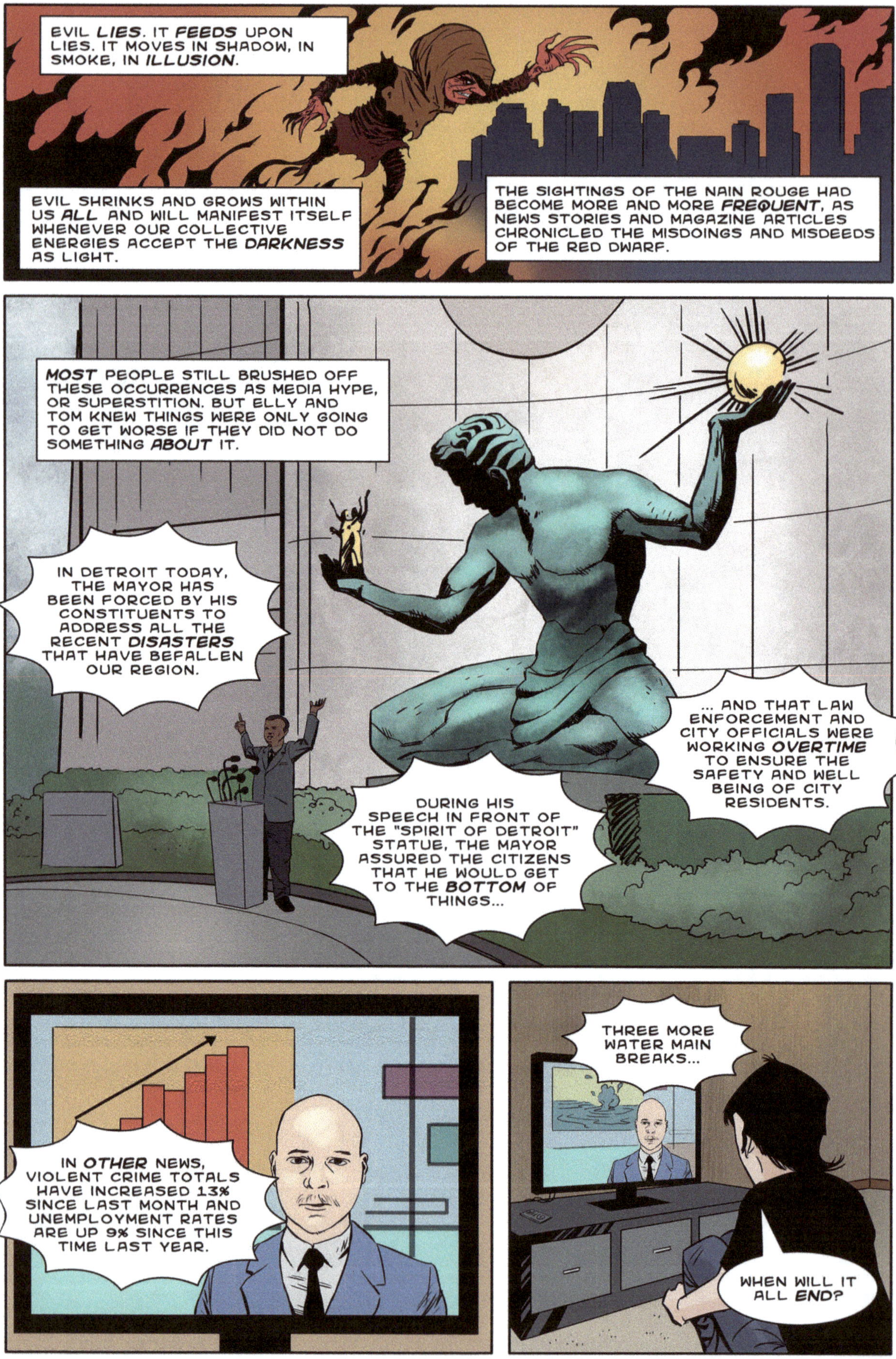

EVIL *LIES*. IT *FEEDS* UPON LIES. IT MOVES IN SHADOW, IN SMOKE, IN *ILLUSION*.
EVIL SHRINKS AND GROWS WITHIN US *ALL* AND WILL MANIFEST ITSELF WHENEVER OUR COLLECTIVE ENERGIES ACCEPT THE *DARKNESS* AS LIGHT.
THE SIGHTINGS OF THE NAIN ROUGE HAD BECOME MORE AND MORE *FREQUENT*, AS NEWS STORIES AND MAGAZINE ARTICLES CHRONICLED THE MISDOINGS AND MISDEEDS OF THE RED DWARF.

MOST PEOPLE STILL BRUSHED OFF THESE OCCURRENCES AS MEDIA HYPE, OR SUPERSTITION. BUT ELLY AND TOM KNEW THINGS WERE ONLY GOING TO GET WORSE IF THEY DID NOT DO SOMETHING *ABOUT* IT.
IN DETROIT TODAY, THE MAYOR HAS BEEN FORCED BY HIS CONSTITUENTS TO ADDRESS ALL THE RECENT *DISASTERS* THAT HAVE BEFALLEN OUR REGION.
DURING HIS SPEECH IN FRONT OF THE "SPIRIT OF DETROIT" STATUE, THE MAYOR ASSURED THE CITIZENS THAT HE WOULD GET TO THE *BOTTOM* OF THINGS...
... AND THAT LAW ENFORCEMENT AND CITY OFFICIALS WERE WORKING *OVERTIME* TO ENSURE THE SAFETY AND WELL BEING OF CITY RESIDENTS.

IN *OTHER* NEWS, VIOLENT CRIME TOTALS HAVE INCREASED 13% SINCE LAST MONTH AND UNEMPLOYMENT RATES ARE UP 9% SINCE THIS TIME LAST YEAR.

THREE MORE WATER MAIN BREAKS...
WHEN WILL IT ALL *END*?

JULY 24TH, UNLESS WE DO SOMETHING SOON!

OK THEN, SO WHAT ABOUT YOUR PLAN?

OH, THAT'S RIGHT, YOU'RE STILL CLUELESS.
HO HO, REAL FUNNY. COME ON, WHAT IS IT?
THIS WHOLE THING, EVERYTHING THAT IS GOING ON, EVERYTHING THAT IS HAPPENING TO US, IT'S ALL ABOUT VENGEANCE; VENGEANCE AND ENERGY.

ENERGY?
REMEMBER THAT SCIENCE PROJECT WE DID LAST MONTH?
IT WAS ALL ABOUT ELECTROMAGNETIC FIELDS AND HOW THE EARTH HAS ITS OWN REALLY HUGE ELECTROMAGNETIC FIELD.

YEAH, SO WHAT?
WHAT DOES THAT HAVE TO DO WITH AN ANCIENT TROLL WHO PLANS ON KILLING US?
AND RECLAIMING THE CITY FOR HIMSELF?

LISTEN, I'VE BEEN DOING SOME RESEARCH AND I THINK I'VE FOUND SOMETHING IMPORTANT.

EARTH SCIENCE
IT'S ALL ABOUT ENERGY. IT'S ALL ABOUT THE ENERGY IN THE EARTH, THE ENERGY WE CREATE.

The earth's natural electromagnetic field has a frequency measured as about 7.8 Hz or Hertz.
This is documented in the Schumann Resonance measured daily in seismology laboratories.
People give off electromagnetic energy as well, their brains emitting alpha frequencies of 7 to 9 Hz. The human brain in a relaxed state will have the same frequency of vibration as the energy field of the earth

YOU'VE LOST ME COMPLETELY EL.

DON'T YOU GET IT?
IT IS ALL ABOUT THE BAD ENERGY THAT'S BEEN BUILDING UP AROUND HERE FOR SO LONG. IT STARTED WITH OUR FOREFATHERS. IT'S BEEN GROWING EVER SINCE.

WE'RE EITHER IN HARMONY OR IN DISCORD WITH THE LAND. WHEN WE DO BAD THINGS AND CREATE BAD ENERGY, THE EARTH RESPONDS NEGATIVELY.
LUTIN IS TIED TO THE LAND. HE'S THE INCARNATION OF BAD ENERGY, OF EVIL!

WE NEED TO RELEASE THE EVIL.
BEFORE OUR ANCESTORS STARTED THIS WHOLE MESS.
I GET IT. WE NEED TO BRING THE HARMONY AND BALANCE BACK TO THE WAY IT WAS.

YES, IT WON'T BE EASY, BUT I THINK IT CAN BE DONE.
LIKE PULLING A PLUG FROM A SOCKET.

YEAH, AS LONG AS WE DON'T GET ELECTROCUTED FIRST!

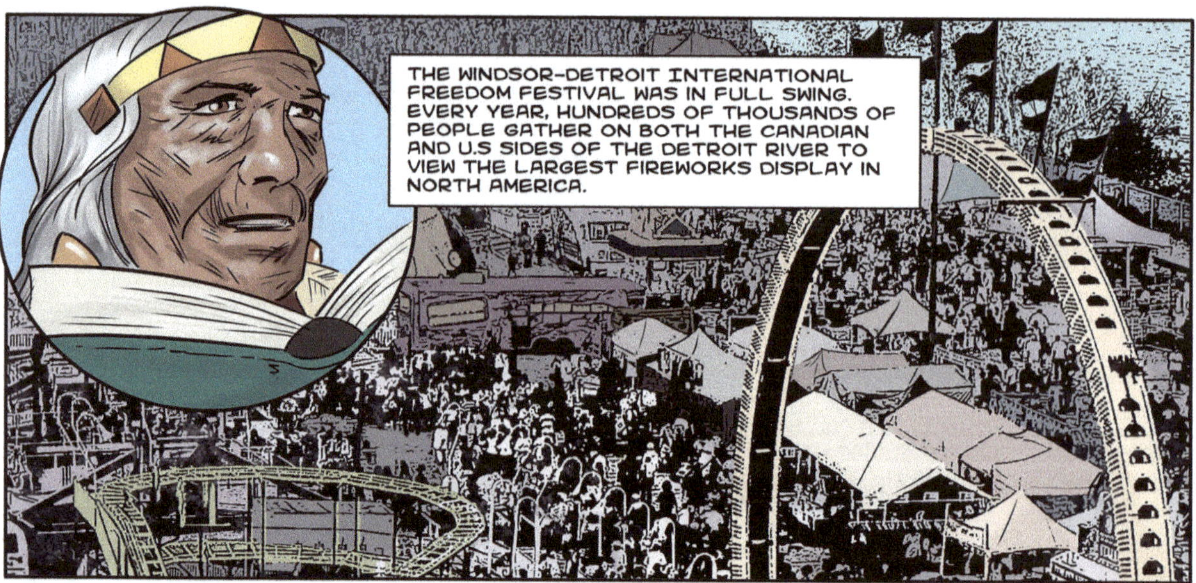

THE WINDSOR-DETROIT INTERNATIONAL FREEDOM FESTIVAL WAS IN FULL SWING. EVERY YEAR, HUNDREDS OF THOUSANDS OF PEOPLE GATHER ON BOTH THE CANADIAN AND U.S SIDES OF THE DETROIT RIVER TO VIEW THE LARGEST FIREWORKS DISPLAY IN NORTH AMERICA.

TOM LOVED TO MEET UP WITH FRIENDS AT THE TECHNO MUSIC FEST, WHERE HE COULD LISTEN TO THE LATEST SOUNDS FROM ALL OVER THE WORLD.

ELLY PREFERRED THE FOOD FESTIVALS, WHERE SHE COULD SAMPLE FOODS AND CULTURES FROM AROUND THE GLOBE.

THE MOST FUN OF ALL WAS THE NIGHT OF FIREWORKS. BOTH SIDES OF THE DETROIT RIVER WERE ALWAYS FILLED WITH EXCITED SPECTATORS, WAITING FOR THE SHOW AT NIGHTFALL.

TOM AND ELLY DID NOT EVEN WANT TO GO DOWNTOWN THIS YEAR, BUT THEY KNEW THAT THEY HAD TO BE THERE JUST IN CASE ANYTHING BAD SHOULD HAPPEN. AND THEY KNEW THAT IT WOULD.
IN FACT, THEY WERE COUNTING ON IT.
ON THE EVENING OF THE FIREWORKS, THEY MET BY THE "JOE LOUIS FIST" STATUE. THIS PUT THEM RIGHT NEAR THE RIVERFRONT, AND DIRECTLY IN THE MIDDLE OF ALL THE ACTION AND EXCITEMENT.

IF LUTIN WAS GOING TO MAKE TROUBLE, THIS WOULD SURELY BE THE SPOT WHERE HE WOULD DO IT.

LUTIN HAD BEEN CAUSING TROUBLE THROUGHOUT THE WEEK OF THE FESTIVAL. TENTS HAD FALLEN DOWN, PORTA-JOHNS HAD BEEN TIPPED OVER AND GARBAGE TOSSED AROUND THE FESTIVAL GROUNDS.
CITY OFFICIALS BLAMED TEENAGERS, BUT ELLY AND TOM KNEW BETTER. THEY KNEW IT WOULD GET WORSE.

HEY, DO YOU FEEL DIFFERENT?
DIFFERENT? WHAT DO YA MEAN?
I CAN'T QUITE EXPLAIN IT. I JUST FEEL DRAINED. LIKE MY SOUL IS SICK.

YEAH, HERE WE ARE, KNOWING THAT WE'RE DOOMED IN A FEW DAYS AND SOMEHOW, IT REALLY DOESN'T SEEM TO MATTER.

I THINK IT'S THE CITY. I NOTICED THAT THESE FEELINGS GET WORSE WHEN WE COME DOWN HERE.

EEEEEEAAAAASSSSSSSSSSSSSSSSSSSSSS!!!!

HELLO CHILDREN.

ENJOYING THE FESTIVAL?

NOT AS MUCH AS WE *COULD* BE.

YOU TWO DON'T LOOK TOO WELL. ARE YOU FEELING A LITTLE DOWN LATELY?

NOT THAT IT'S ANY OF YOUR BUSINESS, BUT YES, WE HAVEN'T BEEN FEELING ALL THAT GREAT.
EVER SINCE WE RAN INTO *YOU*!

WELL, NOT TO *WORRY* MY FRIENDS, IT WILL *ALL* BE OVER SOON.

BY MIDNIGHT TOMORROW ALL OF YOUR TROUBLES WILL BE OVER.

SO HOW ARE YOU GOING TO DO IT?

DO WHAT?
YOU KNOW WHAT HE MEANS! HOW ARE YOU PLANNING TO DESTROY US?

WHY, I TOLD YOU BEFORE, I'M NO KILLER!
BUT I SUPPOSE I CAN SHARE WITH YOU THE MEANS BY WHICH YOU BOTH SHALL PART FROM THIS EARTH.

THE STRANGE WAY THAT YOU BOTH HAVE BEEN FEELING - THAT, MY CHILDREN...
..IS THE BEGINNING OF THE END!

YOUR LIVES WILL NOT END AS ABRUPTLY AS YOU MIGHT HAVE THOUGHT — OR EVEN AS YOU MIGHT HAVE WISHED.
IT IS A SLOW, ABSORBING CURSE THAT ENVELOPS YOU OVER TIME.
THAT IS WHY BY TOMORROW EVENING, THE ELLY AND TOM THAT THE WORLD HAS KNOWN SINCE YOU WERE BORN WILL SIMPLY FADE AWAY...
...DISAPPEAR FOREVER!

OH, LET'S NOT BE SO GLOOMY!

CHEER UP! THE FIREWORKS ARE STARTING!

I KNOW WHAT WILL LIFT YOUR SPIRITS. PERHAPS IF I BROUGHT THE SHOW A LITTLE BIT CLOSER...

...SO YOU CAN BOTH SEE BETTER...

THE BARGE!
GET AWAY FROM THE SHORE!
THE BARGE IS OFF ITS MOORING!

WHAT HAVE YOU DONE?
I AM DOING YOU A FAVOR!
DON'T YOU WANT TO SEE THINGS UP CLOSE?

GET BACK!
TRACY! LOOK OUT!

WHOOSSH!

STOP IT! STOP IT NOW!
I AM SO SORRY THAT YOU DID NOT APPRECIATE MY KIND GESTURE. IN FACT, I'M A BIT HURT.

"KIND GESTURE"? ARE YOU KIDDING ME?
SHOULD I BEGIN THE SHOW AGAIN — EVEN CLOSER THIS TIME?
HEY, THE BARGE IS FLOATING AWAY!

NO!!

WHAT DO I CARE ABOUT THE WELFARE OF STRANGERS?

DON'T DO IT LUTIN. YOU ALREADY HAVE US, WHAT MORE DO YOU WANT?

ALL I ASK IS THAT YOU ALLOW ME THE PLEASURE OF YOUR COMPANY IN YOUR FINAL HOURS.
I WANT TO WATCH YOU DIE, BOTH OF YOU.

ARRGH!
OWW!
WHY CAN'T YOU JUST LET IT HAPPEN? LET US DIE AND BE DONE WITH IT?!

OH MY SWEET, REVENGE IS BEST SERVED COLD...

...AND I INTEND TO SAVOR MY VICTORY.
WATCHING THE TWO OF YOU WITHER AWAY, WHILE I RISE IN TRIUMPH, WELL, THAT IS A MEAL IN WHICH I HAVE LONGED TO PARTAKE.
SO I AM WILLING TO SPARE A FEW OF OUR HUMAN BRETHREN IN ORDER THAT I MIGHT DINE WITH YOU IN YOUR LAST MOMENTS ON EARTH. MAY I DO THAT?

YES.

LOVELY, MY DEARS, LOVELY! I LOOK FORWARD TO SEEING YOU BOTH TOMORROW EVENING.
UNTIL THEN, I BID YOU A FOND ADIEU.

HA HA HA HA HA HA HA HA HA HA HAAA

WELL, I GUESS THIS IS IT.

THE FAIRGROUNDS RESTED ALONGSIDE WOODWARD AVENUE TO THE NORTH AND SOUTH, AND EIGHT MILE ROAD TO THE EAST AND WEST.

THE FINAL EVENT OF THE FESTIVAL WAS TO BE HELD AT THE MICHIGAN STATE FAIRGROUNDS, ON THE NORTHERN BORDER OF DETROIT.

THE FAIRGROUNDS WERE OVER ONE HUNDRED YEARS OLD. THE STATE FAIR GOT ITS PERMANENT HOME IN 1904, AND BY 1905 THE STATE FAIR LAND COMPANY HAD ACQUIRED THE RURAL AREA BETWEEN 7 1/2 AND 8 MILE ROADS, EAST OF WOODWARD AVENUE, THE EDGE THE CITY LIMITS.

FAIRGROUNDS
Welcome
MICHIGAN STATE FAIR
MAIN ENTRANCE
THEIR PLAN WAS TO HAVE DINNER AT THE FAIR, RIDE THE RIDES, SEE THE ATTRACTIONS, AND WAIT FOR *LUTIN* TO SHOW UP.

EVERYBODY *OUT*. FINAL DESTINATION!

I SURE WISH I COULD JUST CURL UP IN A BALL SOMEWHERE.
YEAH.

SKEE-BALL
HELLO, MY FRIENDS!
I THOUGHT, SINCE THIS WAS A SPECIAL OCCASION, I SHOULD DRESS...
...APPROPRIATELY.

WHY NOT TAKE A RIDE ON THE FERRIS WHEEL?
I MEAN, SINCE IT'S YOUR LAST NIGHT ON EARTH, WHY NOT ENJOY YOURSELVES A LITTLE?

SO, WHAT DOES IT FEEL LIKE LITTLE ONES?
TO KNOW THAT IN A FEW MOMENTS YOU WILL BE NO MORE?

WHAT DO YOU CARE?
OH, I CARE VERY MUCH.

I CANNOT TELL YOU HOW MUCH I AM ENJOYING WATCHING YOU TWO SLOWLY WITHER AWAY. I HAVE WAITED OVER 300 YEARS FOR RETRIBUTION.

YOU REALLY ARE W-WICKED.
THAT FACT, I HAVE NEVER DENIED.

ELLY AND TOM FELT COMPLETELY EMPTY. NO ONE SEEMED TO NOTICE THAT THEY WERE BEING SLOWLY DRAINED OF LIFE RIGHT IN THE MIDDLE OF THE MIDWAY. AN ODD, OUT-OF-BODY FEELING CAME OVER THEM.
ELLY WAS DROWNING IN A SEA OF DARKNESS...
TOM REMEMBERED THE WAKE THEY HAD FOR HIS GREAT AUNT, THE CASKET IN THE CORNER AND THE PEOPLE IGNORING THE COLD BODY THAT LAY MOTIONLESS AT ONE END OF THE ROOM.
...SURROUNDED BY THE HAPPINESS OF FESTIVAL GOERS.
TOM FELT LIKE THAT BODY, AN EMPTY SHELL.
SHE COULD ONLY FEEL THE SHIVER OF BLACK WATER FILLING HER LUNGS, DOUSING THE DIMINISHING LIGHT OF HER SPIRIT.

YOU MUST REMEMBER, IT WAS *YOUR* KIND THAT FED ME, NURTURED ME...
... GROOMED ME WITH YOUR LIES, DISTRUST, GREED, VIOLENCE AND ANGER. MADE ME WHAT I AM *TODAY*. AND FOR THAT, I THANK YOU.

OH, AND WHERE DO WE THINK *WE* ARE GOING?

WE NEED TO GET SOME AIR!

I FEEL LIKE I'VE GOT LEAD *WEIGHTS* IN MY SHOES.
LET'S HIDE HERE FOR A SECOND.

TOM, I DON'T THINK I CAN *MAKE* IT.
OH ELLY, COME ON, IT'S JUST A LITTLE BIT FURTHER, WE CAN'T LET HIM WIN, WE JUST *CAN'T*!

SIR! CARE TO TRY A GAME OF CHANCE?

OOOH, I SUPPOSE I CAN TAKE A MOMENT. IT IS MY LUCKY NIGHT!
OON POP!

THUMP!
THUMP!

I'VE BEEN FOLLOWING YOU FOR SOME TIME NOW.

YOU CAN'T GIVE UP NOW. WE'RE ALL COUNTING ON YOU

DR. BEELE!
YES! I HAVE DISTRACTED LUTIN JUST LONG ENOUGH TO GIVE YOU A FIGHTING CHANCE TO DEFEAT HIM.
HE'S PLAYING A GAME AT ANOTHER TENT, BUT HE'LL ONLY BE DIVERTED FOR A FEW MOMENTS.

TIME IS SHORT, YOU MUST GO. JUST REMEMBER, IT IS ALWAYS DARKEST BEFORE THE DAWN...

...AND YOU ARE NOT ALONE!

Exit

DON'T HURRY ON MY ACCOUNT!

Eight Mile
Woodward
KEEP WHAT YOU STEAL AND STEAL WHAT YOU KEEP...

Eight Mile
Woodward
...THE SHEPHERD MUST PAY FOR HIS SINS WITH HIS SHEEP!

AS THEY RAN ACROSS THE INTERSECTION, ELLY AND TOM BEGAN TO HEAR THE FIRST STRIKES OF MIDNIGHT.
UNCONSCIOUSLY, THEY BEGAN COUNTING THE CHIMES IN THEIR HEADS...

ONE

SO! HOW DOES IT FEEL TO DIE?

TWO

TO KNOW THAT IT IS ALL OVER?

THREE

TO KNOW THAT ALL YOU HAVE EVER WORKED FOR AND DREAMED ABOUT IS GONE?

FOUR

WHY DON'T YOU ANSWER?

FIVE

ARE YOU AFRAID TO DIE?

SIX

YOU'RE ASKING IF WE'RE AFRAID TO DIE?
Woodward
Mile

SEVEN

YES! ARE YOU AFRAID TO DIE?
NO...
Woodward
Mile

EIGHT

Woodward
Eight Mile
...ARE YOU?

NINE

WHAT HAVE YOU DONE?!
IT'S NOT WHAT WE DID, IT'S WHAT YOU DID!

TEN

YOU CROSSED THE LINE!
YOU THOUGHT YOU WERE HEADED WEST, WHEN YOU WERE HEADED NORTH!

ELEVEN

SO MUCH FOR BEING IN TOUCH WITH THE LAND.
YOU LEFT THE CITY!

TWELVE

EEEEEAAAASSSSSSSSSSSSSSSSSSS!!

Woodward
Eight Mile
KA-FROOOM!

YOUR PLAN -- IT WORKED!
I KNEW SOMETHING GOOD WOULD HAPPEN IF WE COULD JUST GET HIM OUT OF THE CITY LIMITS.

LIKE PULLING A PLUG FROM A SOCKET!
Eight Mi
Woodward

BRILLIANT PLAN! YOU GUESSED RIGHT ABOUT THE SOURCE OF HIS POWER.
AND THAT HIS POWER WAS HIS WEAKNESS.

YES! AS STEWARD OF THE STRAITS, THE NAIN ROUGE WAS TIED INTO THE LAND.
HE DREW HIS STRENGTH FROM THE LAND ON WHICH DETROIT WAS FOUNDED. ONCE HE STEPPED OFF HIS CLAIMED TERRITORY, CROSSING OVER EIGHT MILE ROAD, HE UNPLUGGED HIS OWN POWER CORD.

YOU TOOK A BIG CHANCE.
THANK GOODNESS WE GUESSED RIGHT!

WOW, I FEEL BETTER THAN I HAVE IN WEEKS.
ME TOO!

WELL, THE FAIR IS CLOSING.
TIME TO GO HOME.

YES, TIME TO GO HOME.

ELLY WOKE IN THE MORNING AS IF IT HAD ALL BEEN A DREAM; THE MUSEUM, THE FESTIVAL, THE STATE FAIRGROUNDS.
SHE GOT OUT OF BED FEELING FATIGUED BUT HAPPY...

...LIKE AFTER WORKING ALL DAY IN HER MOM'S GARDEN.

GUESS WHAT?

I DON'T KNOW, WHAT?
THEY CALLED ME BACK TO WORK. I START MONDAY!
Chef

WOW!

HEY ELLY! COME ON IN!
I'M HELPING MY MOM GET READY FOR HER NEW BUSINESS.

THAT SOUNDS GREAT, DID SHE GET A NEW JOB?
SORT OF. SHE'S SETTING UP HER OWN PHOTOGRAPHY BUSINESS. SHE HAS FOUR CLIENTS ALREADY! THE FRONT STUDY IS GOING TO BE HER NEW OFFICE.

THAT'S REALLY COOL! OH, MY DAD GOT CALLED BACK TO WORK TOO.
I GUESS THINGS ARE LOOKING UP FOR EVERYBODY.

YEAH, THINGS SURE SEEM DIFFERENT SINCE LAST NIGHT.
SHHH!

SO EL, HOW LONG DO YOU THINK THIS WILL LAST?
THE GOOD STUFF, I MEAN.

I DON'T KNOW TOMMY. IT MAY BE UP TO US.
I GUESS THE GOOD STUFF LASTS AS LONG AS WE WANT IT TO.

THE END

FOR NOW...

OUR SUPPORTERS

THIS GRAPHIC NOVEL WOULD NOT HAVE BEEN POSSIBLE WITHOUT THE GENEROUS SUPPORT OF ALL OUR KICKSTARTER BACKERS. INCLUDED BELOW ARE BACKERS FROM THE "SUPPORTER" REWARD LEVEL AND UP:

Adrianna Melchior
Anita Heap
Bernhard and Marta Bastian
Bo Kaburov
Bugaboo Tear Oncology Raffle
Carol Johnson
Chuck Deeds
Daniel P. Johnson
Danny McCarthy
Dave Crilley
Dean Stevenson
Debi and Dave Keeling
Diane Whitt
Donna Herrle
Don Tanner
Ellen S. Abramowitz
Fran Taterelli
Francis Grunow
Gary E. Baker
Greg Swartz
Jacob & Alex Myers
Janaree Nagel
Jeff Hensley
Jeffrey Neracher
Jennifer Kockler
Jerry Winans

Jim Guido
Joel Pritchard
John Funk
Katrina Furlong
Kenny Hemler
Kevin Mercury
Kirk Karamanian
Kristiann Grove
Komorn Laww, PLLC
Lauren Schafer
Linda Bateman
Martin Klebba
Matthew Dibble
Matthew Sakey
Megan Torrance
Michelle Bauer-Mosher
Mike Budziak
Nick Ellis
Pat and Earl Crilley
Patrick Callaghan
Paul Martin
Paul Tobin
Rod Grozenski
Roger Beckett
Ross Gordon
Ryan Keeling
Steve Smiscik
Teresa Huntoon
The Austin Family
The Gordon Family
The Zimmerman Family
Todd Palmer
Tom Gatliff
Tracey Banghart
William Bastian

1898
INDIAN TERRITORY
Will Firemaker is a Cherokee Blacksmith who is finding out that the legends of the Tribe are true, and they're telling him he must replace his best friend from the animal kingdom as a guardian of the people.
NEXT: THE BOBCAT REVEALED!
THE BOBCAT
CALIBER
AVAILABLE AT YOUR LOCAL COMIC SHOP OR AT CALIBERCOMICS.COM

DARK FRONTIER

A POST-APOCALYPTIC TALE FOR MAD MAX FANS!

NOW AVAILABLE FROM

www.calibercomics.com

FROM ONE OF THE PREMIER INDEPENDENT PUBLISHERS
CALIBER COMICS
GRAPHIC NOVELS · COMICS
DIGITAL BOOKS · NOVELS
WWW.CALIBERCOMICS.COM

www.ingramcontent.com/pod-product-compliance
Lightning Source LLC
Chambersburg PA
CBHW041158100726
47911CB00016B/786